The Duchess of Pontsylvania

Being the history of fifty-five months
in the life of a Ruritanian gentlewoman

Translated from the original manuscript

by

Kristin Rose

First Printing 2023
ISBN: 979-8-9877737-0-3
Publisher:
Kristin Rose
Windsor, Vermont

This is a work of fiction. Any resemblance between characters depicted herein and actual persons, including shared names, is entirely coincidental. The Ruritanian County of Eisenstein has absolutely nothing to do with the municipality of Bayerisch Eisenstein (termed only "Eisenstein" before 1951), located in the Free State of Bavaria in southeastern Germany on the border of Czechoslovakia, 214 kilometers from the Austrian border and 311 kilometers from Liechtenstein. Egypt is real and although it is much changed since the 1890s, if you ever get the chance, you should go there.

❧ Table of Contents ❧

Cover of American edition of
The Prisoner of Zenda, 1895

Author's Note

I send my gratitude to the spirit of Anthony Hope (Sir Anthony Hope Hawkins) for his creation of the classic works on which this literary trifle is based. It is said he was inspired to write his Ruritanian tale on seeing a photograph of King George V of the United Kingdom and British Dominions beside his cousin, the unfortunate Tsar Nicholas II of Russia, and noting their familial resemblance was such that they appeared to be twins. It is also said he conceived the idea of *Zenda* in December of 1893. As the book was published in April of 1894, we should all be duly impressed. I don't know how many times I've read and enjoyed the *Prisoner of Zenda / Rupert of Hentzau* duology.* It is, in my opinion, one of the silliest things ever put on paper. This does not make me love it any less.

I do confess I have cheated on Sir Anthony in not describing the 18th century chateau at Zenda as constructed directly against the moat surrounding the old castle. As a homeowner I just think this a preposterously bad idea, though it did serve as a handy device to enable Rupert von Hentzau to jump out Antoinette de Mauban's bedroom window without breaking a leg. And sure, according to the Prove Me Wrong Department, somebody out there somewhere in Europe probably did build a chateau this way during the 18th century. I look forward to hearing about it.

Who does this?

I have also taken the liberty of spelling the name(s) of the king and his elusive *doppelgänger* cousin as "Rudolph" rather than "Rudolf." I can speculate "Rudolph Elphberg" might have appeared an awkward option to Sir Anthony but I consider it an opportunity not to be missed.

I must also confess the Austrian cigar lighter mentioned in the text is an anachronism, not having come into production for another decade following the publication of *Rupert of Hentzau*, at least as far as I've been able to determine. I beg suspension of disbelief with regard to this one false note in an otherwise entirely credible narrative.

—*KR*

**The Prisoner of Zenda* and *Rupert of Hentzau* are sometimes referred to as two parts of Hope's "Ruritanian Trilogy." The third book in this trilogy, *The Heart of Princess Osra*, is a prequel; a series of stories regarding an 18th century Ruritanian princess, taking place many generations prior to the events of *Zenda* and *Hentzau*.

"Faith, Madame, had your eyes been no more deadly than your shooting I had not been in this scrape."

—Rupert von Hentzau,
The Prisoner of Zenda by Anthony Hope

❧ Preface ❧

Text of a letter accompanying the manuscript

My So Beloved Melisande,

I have just heard of the passing away at Antibes of our dear Flavia Grosvenor, formerly Flavia von Turmen and Elphberg who once reigned as our Queen in Strelsau. I, too, have lived out my days. The end draws near. I have known greater happiness in my life than is granted to many in this world. I have also known privation, horrors and painful losses, as have we all. We have seen the old order fall away. The sun has long since set on the Ruritanian monarchy and all men stand as peers regardless of their birth, yet still we are blessed that the heart of what was once the County of Eisenstein remains in our possession. As you know, all the jewels of the Eisens and Plinths were sacrificed to bring our family and such others as we could manage to rescue through the great conflagration that left much of Europe burned to the ground a decade past. However the ring which remains today upon my left hand is of far greater significance to me than any of those. When at last you take it from my finger, you will find this inscription inside the band: *AETERNVS vTVRMEN*. It is my pleasure to leave it to you, my Dear, and I trust you will treasure it as fondly as I have.

Everything of my life's joys and sorrows have I shared with you save for this: the true story of my marriage to

Gerhard Richter von Plinth, Duke of Pontsylvania, and how that marriage was brought to its end. I now surrender these pages to only your eyes, that I may depart with no secrets from you. If Max had survived the Great War and was living still, I could not do this. Only to you may I now reveal this passage in my history never spoken of for over half a century. You have been at my side through the wars and thus you have an idea of the measure of my mettle, yet still I fear you will be shocked to read of my deeds done in earlier days when you were not yet born and Max too young to remember. I can only say I have passed nearly six decades in striving to make recompense for my sins. I beg your kind understanding.

Consigned to you with my great love,

Mother

December, 1954

I. I am wed to Pontsylvania

My husband Gerhard Richter von Plinth, incumbent of the Duchy of Pontsylvania in the Royal Dominion of Ruritania, was in my estimation a horrible man. His companions at hunting and cardplay might well have said he was a fine fellow and there is some reason to believe he may have been loved by at least one person in addition to his mother, but these admirers were not married to him. That misfortune was mine alone.

Seven weeks after my nineteenth birthday, we were introduced at a lavish ball arranged between my dear father, the Count Sylvandre Heldenhaft von Eisen, and Agathe, Dowager Duchess of Pontsylvania. In my youthful folly I believed myself quite ready to marry and the Duke of Pontsylvania looked to be a highly desirable catch. He appeared as a mature and sophisticated man to my eyes, though he was not yet forty. He had ascended rather early to his rank when his father departed life in middle age, having been struck with a stray bullet and instantly dispatched whilst enjoying himself among a perhaps excessively large gathering of his peers participating in a duck shoot hosted by His Grace the Grand Duke Wilhelm von Ormstein in Bohemia. A union with Pontsylvania would bring elevation to the highest level of aristocratic society, a notion which greatly pleased my father, not for the sake of any avarice or ambition but due to the profound sense of my future security he imagined it to convey. In addition to Pontsylvania's own qualities, he seemed thoroughly taken with me, demonstrating all the most attentive of courtesies while presenting a series of tokens and gifts of incrementally increasing value and significance. He spent much time with my father as well and demonstrated a lively interest in our County of Eisenstein despite that his own holdings were greater by far. He made his proposal in the charming setting of the Rose Garden behind the Royal Library. I had great hopes of Gerhard von Plinth.

On the first day of June in the year 1893, at the culmination of a whirlwind of not quite six months, we descended the vast steps of the National Cathedral of Strelsau following a seemingly interminable ceremony during which I thought I might die of starvation. As I ascended to my seat in the bridal carriage, my long veil of white lace, laden with rose petals, became tightly snagged in the hinge of the door. Not only did my hasty efforts to free it cause a rent in the delicate fabric, this tear was left marked with a stain of black grease. Of course nothing so inconsequential could distress me on my wedding day.

Laughing in the highest of spirits, I lifted off the Eisenstein Tiara to detach the spoiled veil as it shed scarlet petals all over my dress and Pontsylvania's trousers. I quickly bundled the several yards of lace into a ball which I stowed away beneath the seat. After replacing the tiara around the piled crown of thick, dark braids atop my head, I turned to him with a smile only to perceive, to my surprise, he was annoyed. Although I did not know it then, that moment was the First Sign.

The boat-like open carriage was a perfectly maintained relic of the prior century, lacquered in Prussian blue with the arms of Pontsylvania painted in gold leaf upon the doors, the seats covered with wine red plush. We were on display for all Strelsau as a team of four white horses drew us in a slow and halting progress along the Grand Boulevard through a sea of waving handkerchiefs, flowers raining down from high windows and balconies as we passed below. I reflected for a moment upon my cousin, the Honorable Manfred von Eisen Klench. Now entirely safe from his relentless campaign to persuade my father to grant him my hand, I was flushed with relief at the final ending of that threat which had loomed over me for years. No fate of mine on Earth, I felt quite sure, would be worse than a life attached to Manfred Klench. To this day I know that belief was not misplaced. However I would soon be disappointed to find I had come only so far as from fire to frying pan.

But a few moments after we passed the towering iron gates of the Royal Palace of Ruritania, I spied at the forefront of the crowd a tall young woman in a blue figured dress and straw hat with velvet roses, her chestnut hair in long plaits. I started up in recognition as she rushed forward, lifting a bunch of white lilacs. She cried, "God bless you, Your Grace!"

It was Katerina Manx, our steward's daughter from the Eisenstein lands, dear friend of my childhood. I caught the posy from her outstretched hand, calling back to her, "Thank you, Kitty Dear!" She was immediately left behind as we rolled on and the carriage filled with the sweet, pungent scent of the lilacs. I arranged the fragrant blooms within the circlet of the Eisenstein Tiara.

This addition, though certainly festive, may have appeared rather informal. Turning once again to my husband, I saw him frowning and just opening his mouth to speak when a yellow rose landed upon the top of his head and stuck there. Quite naturally as anyone would have, I burst into peals of laughter. He flung the rose violently off as if it were some viper or poisonous spider, then turned to stare relentlessly forward with a wooden face. I felt a momentary urge to make some sort of apology but then realized that would be just too absurd, and so I said nothing.

I did not look to him again until we arrived at the great house which would henceforth be my home, where the orchestra was tuning up in the ballroom, the long buffet loaded with delicacies, crowded bottles of wine breathing in the pantry, tulip glasses arranged on fifty trays. My countenance a mask of quiet dignity, my sides aching from long confinement in the tightest corset, my hunger gnawing, I recalled I had a few powers available to me as the newly made Duchess Hilda Marie von Eisen and von Plinth of Pontsylvania, powers even beyond the choosing of draperies. I resolved to send for Kitty Manx at the earliest opportunity.

We entered the ballroom where immense glittering chandeliers had been lit and raised high into the arch of a domed ceiling across which painted cherubim frolicked among clouds tinted pink by a perpetual dawn. To Pontsylvania I said, "I beg you to excuse me for a moment, my Dear."

He replied, "Not now. It is imperative we form the receiving line before The Royals arrive.

"Oh please, Gerhard, I will not survive the receiving line without a few moments of retirement. I can't imagine The Royals will rush to our door without taking more than a few such moments for themselves. I assure you I shall be prompt." With these words and a conciliatory smile, I hastened away. As I passed from the room, I noted Manfred von Eisen Klench in conversation with two other gentleman, his dark eyes boldly following me.

The Royals did eventually arrive after we had been standing for perhaps another hour, and so I was introduced to His Majesty Rudolph V, King of Ruritania. The ceremony of his coronation was yet in preparation, the old King having passed away less than a year previously. He was a tall, fair gentleman with piercing blue eyes, a narrow Roman nose, the wavy auburn hair of the Elphbergs and a great bushy red beard like a pair of enormous mutton chop sideburns not quite meeting at the end of his chin. He congratulated Pontsylvania heartily, slapping him on the back and inviting him to "come out after some boar as soon as you've tired of honeymooning."

Following the King came his younger half brother Michael Elphberg, Grand Duke of Strelsau. He was of lesser stature than Rudolph with features suggestive of Tatar blood: a short nose, straight black hair and eyes so dark one could barely discern the pupils, his beard confined to a small moustache above a closely trimmed goatee. Indeed they looked nothing alike and one must assume Michael took after his mother. He was as self-contained as his brother was effusive, simply clasping first my husband's hand and then my own whilst making a slight bow and twice repeating, "I congratulate you and wish you the best." He did also look me directly in the eye, yet only momentarily. His grip was firm, deliberate and brief, and no sooner had I uttered the words "Thank you kindly, Your Grace," than he moved on.

I was next introduced to the King's cousin, Her Royal Highness Princess Flavia von Turmen of Gothe-Saxeberg. She was most gracious and stated I must come to Tea at Court while the aforementioned hunting expedition with the King went on. Flavia was a breathtakingly beautiful woman, of noble bearing and statuesque in figure. Her porcelain complexion was sweetly dappled with tiny freckles across the cheeks and nose whilst a mass of flaming copper curls she carried bound atop her head encircled in a tiara consisting of two narrow bands, each set with a row of diamonds and pearls. She wore a gown of pale blue satin, simple yet elegantly cut, with a modest array of additional diamonds. She could easily have dressed for the occasion so as to completely overshadow me, the bride, and I could only conclude she deliberately had not done so. She had arrived from Gothe-Saxberg only a fortnight previously to take up residence for an indefinite stay within the Royal Palace. It was widely speculated a betrothal with the King was under consideration but there had been no announcement. I imagined she was a woman whose life consisted entirely of duty and wondered for a just moment, while feeling a quick stab of anxiety, just how much I might be required to become like her in this regard.

As the ordeal of the receiving line drew near its end, I inevitably found myself confronted with the Honorable Manfred Klench. He lifted my hand to impudently examine the sapphire encircled with diamonds, the Star of Pontsylvania. "What a pretty little thing, Madam Cousin," he murmured with a lift of supercilious black brows. I felt his revolting moustache on the back of my hand where it lingered too long. Even the limp fabric of his shirt cuff managed to brush across my fingers like an unwanted caress. He addressed Pontsylvania. "Well, Plinth, you have won the Grand Prize. I trust you will prove worthy."

"I thank you, Klench," my new husband replied, standing all the more erect and thrusting out his chest in the manner of a pouter pigeon. I perceived with dismay he was flattered by this marginally rude remark. "As a new kinsman to this house, we hope you will call on us soon."

"You may depend upon it. I shall be pleased." Manfred bowed low before casting me the most fleeting final glance in which his eyes betrayed a smoldering resentment. I still imagined, however, that I was safe.

Only once that evening did he attempt to claim a dance. My brother Raoul cut him out immediately, saying, "I'm sure you will forgive me, Manfred. As I return so shortly to my post, I must monopolize my sister's attention while I may."

As we glided away to the opening strains of *Die Lorelei*, I said, "You know he hates it when you address him man-to-man as 'Manfred' instead of 'Klench.' As if he's still a boy."

"Ha!" Raoul, six years my senior, had ever been my protector. "Never more than 'Manfred' to me. Those spit curls he affects are quite vile, don't you think?" Raoul, like myself, had thick dark hair, a lock of vigorous natural curls spilling down over the center of his forehead.

"Well I'll not have to marry him. You know there was a time when I was positively terrified; he's so ingratiated with Father."

"Even moreso Aunt Olympia. She's tried her utmost on behalf of her dear boy. Tried far too hard. And I've done all I could do for you in counter, if largely through the post. And so it's not to happen. Auntie O must look elsewhere for some poor debutante to marry her horrid boy, and you're a duchess."

"Oh, you know I care very little about all that. In fact I fear it may become a bore."

"Oh yes, Hildie Dear, I know."

"But the Eisenstein lands are safe and our people will remain well provided for."

"Pontsylvania must keep to his word on that. Father and I have established his commitments in the clearest possible terms. Come what may, it is not your burden, Hilda. If there's ever the slightest hint he intends not to meet his obligations, promise you'll write to me at once."

"I do promise. But you don't really think that's possible?"

"I only suggest you be watchful and never be taken in by any excuse. The great Duchy of Pontsylvania can easily afford our little Eisenstein, Hildie, I do assure you."

Later, following upon a festive midnight supper and the departures of many of our guests, I strolled with Raoul through the walled garden among graceful fountains, sheltering arbors, a labyrinth of paths. There were scattered lanterns of colored glass, the candles within them burning low. I was inexpressibly weary.

"Not bad, all this," he said.

"It is very lovely," I replied, "but I'll appreciate it all the better on another day when my feet are not on fire."

"Just a little farther along," he said, "I want to sit where we'll be quite alone."

We settled on a serpentine iron bench in the farthest corner of the wall. He passed his arm around my shoulders. "Hilda, there is more I must say to you tonight, while I still can."

"You go tomorrow, then?"

"I go."

"Is it so very interesting in Constantinople?"

"Oh, most diverting indeed. You've no idea. But I may not continue there much longer."

"Where to, then?"

"Cairo, I expect."

"Oh, even farther away!"

"Alas, yes. I'll no longer be able to entrain for Strelsau by the Orient Express as I've been accustomed to do. It's going to mean taking ship across the Mediterranean. But if any dire need arises, even threatens to arise, I will come home."

"But that would take quite some time."

"It would. Which is why I ask you to listen to me tonight, very seriously. Do not allow yourself to become complacent about Manfred.

"But surely I'm out of his reach now."

"In one sense you are, but I live in the world of men and I know things you do not know. I assure you he's as vindictive now as he ever was. Remember when he was ten, what he did to my dog in his little fit of pique."

"Dear God. I try never to think of that."

"Do not forget it. He has not changed. He will never change."

Resting my heavy head on his shoulder, I sighed. "Poor Aunt Olympia."

"Yes, poor Auntie O. She's a silly woman but she doesn't deserve whatever sorrows Manfred is bound to bring down upon her. And Hildie, there is one other warning I must make to you. When you write to me, don't ever put to paper a single word you would not want your husband to see."

"What? Are you quite serious?"

"Oh, absolutely. I'll enlarge upon it. Do not put your name to anything you wouldn't want printed in the newspapers. You'll remember this, Hilda?"

"I'll remember."

We rested there without speech for a time, breathing the fragrances of the flowers, listening to the flutter of birds and rustling small creatures in the shrubberies, the soft plashing of fountains. One by one, the guttering candle flames began to fail and vanish. Fireflies winked among the leaves and drifted across the path like floating sparks. In the distance, the rooftops and chimneys of the great house loomed high in silhouette before a dark blue velvet sky sprinkled with stars.

"Do you know what is more lovely to me than all this?" I asked.

"What, Hilda?"

"The hills, fields and forests of our Eisenstein."

A tall man approached us from the direction of the house, a long-legged silhouette in the gloom, gravel crunching softly beneath his shoes. The smoke of his thin cigar intruded upon the scents of the garden, the tip glowing orange in the dark. It was Pontsylvania. He stood before me and held out his hand. Raoul rose, bent to kiss my cheek, bowed to my husband, and left me there.

II. Duchess of Pontsylvania

In the surroundings of my new life there was all that was pleasant and comfortable, yet shadows soon gathered around me. Pontsylvania was, I suppose, what was considered a true gentleman in the decade in which we then found ourselves. He was at least a personable man and he was not a brute, but the weight of his expectations suffocated me. I would not, could not, keep him happy. He would have me be as an ornament to his person, always to be beautifully turned out, by his side and supporting him in all things. I was not to reveal my knowledge of any number of unladylike topics including, yet certainly not limited to: horse and dog breeding, butchering of game and cleaning of fish, nursing of the sick or wounded, how to get bloodstains out of laundry, sweating, politics, the diverse religious doctrines of the world and how *knackwurst* are assembled. In addition to such constraints, I was given to understand my opinions on virtually any matter were of no value, and there seemed little in the way of activities he approved of my partaking in which felt worthwhile to me. He was not as he had appeared previous to our wedding and it was quite dreadful. I had never imagined such a life.

Pontsylvania answered my numberless little transgressions with cold disapproval, with silences, with disappearances. The sympathy that had grown between us during our brief courtship began to slip away in but a few months' time. I missed my father's town house and manor, the ways of our family and all that had been my life within the family von Eisen.

Raoul and I exchanged letters which took weeks to pass between us. I wrote with caution, taking care to make no open issue of my disappointment though he knew me well and in all likelihood could read between my lines. My beloved father I sought to protect from any knowledge of my regrets, knowing he had meant all for the best.

My apartments in Strelsau's Pontsylvania House were large and commodious, consisting of bedroom, dressing room, sitting and writing rooms. I was attended by two personal maids: Elsa, who managed my suite of rooms and acted as my secretary, and Henriette, who cared for my clothing and shoes, dressed me and did my hair. I took a childish pleasure at first in arranging my furnishings, ordering installation of a flowered carpet that filled the bedroom, and causing the draperies and hangings of the bed to be replaced in combinations of peach colored velvet and cream satin brocaded with vines full of rose blossoms. I was soon to realize, however, this bedroom would not be my private refuge nor was the vast bed to be as the nest of peace and security my bed had been at home. It was instead the scene of my awkward intimacies with Pontsylvania.

He did have the good grace not to visit me every night, or at least he had his men friends and their manly activities of fencing, target shooting, horse racing, cards and convivial drinking that served to occupy his attention and many late evenings. He was invited periodically to go out with the King's hunting parties. These sorties would last several days at a time during which I was left with relief to my own devices while he spent many happy hours with his fellow gentlemen, crashing through the underbrush on horseback in fervent pursuit of the occasional bear and untold numbers of unfortunate boar, deer and elk.

During one of these absences I had a comfortable couch brought in and placed in a corner of my dressing room. The high wall at the foot of this couch was hung with a tapestry depicting a wooded mountainside, the ruin of an ancient castle in the distance. It was not literally a depiction of the Eisenstein lands but so very like it, I could pretend. This became my true place of rest and I would sleep there when Pontsylvania was away. Of course there was no need to mention to him this minor domestic detail regarding furniture arrangement, and as my dressing room entry was not a door but a passage lined with drawers and cabinets, he had no occasion to lay eyes upon it. For months I would naively assume he knew nothing about it.

I received the following letter from Kitty Manx:

Madam Hilda von Eisen and von Plinth

Your Grace,

I am highly honored by your request for me to enter your employment and your father the Count graciously releases me to go to you as I choose. However my own dear father Everard Manx is now confined to his bed having suffered a fall from a horse, news I have no doubt will be grievous to you. I cannot leave his side in good conscience. I do pledge to make myself available to you when his condition improves.

Yours sincerely,

Katerina Manx

This was bitter in several ways. I had wanted Kitty with me and was disappointed. I was sorely grieved to learn of her father, our loyal and capable steward Everard Manx, coming to harm. I was also both sad and irritated that my dear Kitty was so distanced by my pretentious marriage she felt required to write me this horribly stilted letter and address me as "Madam Hilda von Eisen and von Plinth, Your Grace."

When next visiting my father at our town house in Strelsau, I inquired about Everard Manx. Father of course was already aware of Mr. Manx's accident. He told me Kitty's elder brother, Reynard, was fulfilling the duties of stewardship and this arrangement would likely prove permanent given the extremity of Mr. Manx's condition. Realizing Kitty's letter had presented the situation with undue optimism, I felt the strongest impulse to travel to Eisenstein without delay.

On returning home, I sought Pontsylvania that I might speak to him of my wish to visit the Manx family. I was directed to the lesser drawing room where he was lingering alone, having just overseen the installation of a new acquisition. This was a stuffed pure white peacock with its tail unfurled, displayed behind glass in a vast shadow box with a gilt rococo frame within which it stood upon a bed of green silk grass before a painted scene of *verdure*. I had seen peacocks before in the gardens of the Royal Palace, but never a white one. I believe I would have found it quite breathtaking to behold had it not been dead.

In response to my news, he said, "But surely this matter is beneath your concern."

"I think not. These are our people. I have known them all my life."

"Hilda, your place is here while I am here. When next I leave Strelsau on business for a fortnight or more, you may go then if you still wish it."

"Can you say when that is likely to occur?"

"No," he replied, "I really have no idea."

After an interval of silence during which I was aware of holding my face very still, I said, "There is another matter."

"And what is that?"

"It is about my cousin, Manfred Klench."

"Eisen Klench?"

"Klench, really. My father, my brother and I know the addition of 'von Eisen' to be an affectation adopted by his mother on the unfortunate occasion of her widowhood, which preceded Manfred's birth by several months and at which time my father generously offered her residence at the Eisenstein manor house. Eisen had never been her name, only a name reflecting that which she unreasonably wished to possess."

"Is that her own explanation?"

"No, of course she would never admit to that. She would state some nonsense about honoring her ancestry. She is my mother's sister and their maiden name was Eider, but their great grandmother had been an Eisen."

"And what did you want to tell me about Manfred von Eisen Klench?

"During the exchange of courtesies on our wedding day, your intentions were undoubtedly kind in inviting my cousin to call here. I had not assumed he would in actuality presume to do so, but I now understand it has happened."

Pontsylvania inclined his head in acknowledgment of this yet I detected a faint hint of mockery in his expression. I pressed on: "I must make you aware Manfred's company is quite intolerable to me. I would very much prefer never to be obliged to sit down with him *en famille* in my own home or to join in any intimate gathering at which he is also present."

His mouth tightened into a small, bleak smile. "And this is because . . ?"

"My aunt, Manfred's mother, had her heart set for many years on a match between Manfred and myself. He was greatly influenced by her in this, such that he took it for granted since we were children."

"Of course I am well aware he had also addressed his suit to your father, yet he has shown himself a gentleman in defeat."

"I have known Manfred Klench from childhood and he has never been a gentleman in defeat about anything, only pretended to be when it suits his purpose. He cannot be trusted."

"Can it possibly have escaped your notice, my Dear, that I am one of the most powerful men in Ruritania? You should feel entirely safe under my protection."

"But Manfred is devious and vindictive. His only moral criterion is whether or not his wrongdoings will escape detection. I beg you to take heed of this."

"Is it not curious then your father has not felt any such need to warn me off? Indeed, when I visited at Eisenstein and your cousin was on the estate, I recall he made rather a point of seeing that we were introduced."

"My father is certainly a man for taking care to observe all the expected courtesies among gentlemen. However I must add that Manfred became adept long ago at hiding the darker side of his nature from those of the older generations, including his own mother. It is his contemporaries who know what he is capable of. My father has been quite naïve on the matter and Manfred of course until recently had every reason for making sure to keep it so."

"Well, Hilda, as my wife, I'm afraid you will have to place your faith in my judgement. And as for any passing social awkwardness that may arise in the presence of your cousin should he appear here again in the future, you can always do what you women do, and excuse yourself."

Just to the right of his head on the marble mantle shelf behind him stood a horrible gilded sculptural clock depicting the struggles of Laocoön. The startling thought came to my mind that should Pontsylvania happen to pass away before myself, I would have it disposed of immediately.

I soon fell pregnant.

III. Pontsylvania is momentarily pleased with me

My condition reduced me to a wretched state for quite some time. After hiding in my apartments for a fortnight while gaining certainty of my the nature of my ailment, I forced myself to dress and went to speak with my husband in his study, the room he would retire to after dinner on his evenings at home. I had not considered in advance he would likely be smoking, as he in fact was, and how that would affect me. I tapped at the door and entered, was struck with the stink of burning tobacco, sank into one of the leather armchairs which flanked a tiled fireplace and attempted to breathe though my mouth.

He looked up from his writing after a time, replaced his pen in its stand, took up his fat smoldering cigar, drew in and expelled a noxious plume. "You look remarkably pale, Hilda. You are still ill, are you not? Should you be up?"

I pressed a cold palm to my clammy brow. "I am not really ill. I do feel very ill indeed but I'm actually not."

"Whatever do you mean?"

"I mean there is to be a child coming to us in the winter and it's only my condition which makes me feel as I do."

"Why, my Dear! This is excellent news!" He knocked the end off the cigar in a horrid brass ashtray in the shape of an elephant's apparently amputated foot, arose from the desk and came to place his heavy hands upon my shoulders. "I am positively delighted, Hilda! But you must rest and we'll have the doctor in."

"I don't think I need the doctor, really. I believe the sickness is normal and it should pass off in time."

"We'll have him in nonetheless. And you should be in bed."

"I think not bed, at least not all the time, but I will remain in my apartments for a while and I must send for Cook. If I confide to her my condition, surely she can provide me with nourishment I can tolerate. Broths, bread, tisanes and such."

"Very well," he said, "Let me escort you back. Really my Dear, I am most pleased; most pleased indeed. You must take every care."

"I will. Of course I will." Planting my hands on the arms of the chair, I struggled to my feet as he placed a solicitous hand beneath my elbow.

We progressed but a few steps toward the door before he suddenly halted and I felt his hand drop away. "There is point I've been waiting to take up with you when you recovered, but since you're not ill, I think I should mention it now."

I yearned for the fresh air beyond the door. "Yes, what is it?"

"These Manx people at Eisenstein. You sent funds to them in an extravagant amount and did not consult me."

"Did I need to consult you?"

"If you had, I would have objected. Perhaps that is why you did not."

"What possible objection could there be, Gerhard? I'm sure the sum was virtually nothing to a man of your station."

"It is a matter of principle."

"The Manxes are in extreme difficulty. I've been unable to appear at Eisenstein at all and it now appears likely I may not visit there for a long time yet. The funds will help to pay for help in nursing Mr. Manx or for whatever they might employ to ease his suffering. As I'm unable to be present and assist myself . . ."

"Thank God you are not," he interrupted. "Can you not see that would be most unseemly?"

"No. No, I cannot see that at all. But this gift in their time of terrible strife has been all I'm able to do for them, so I've done it."

"These people are your father's responsibility, not ours."

"Yes they certainly are, and my father will indeed provide for them, being the good man he is. My gift was a means to demonstrate how deeply I care about their plight despite my absence."

"I see we cannot agree on this. In any event, I forbid

any further transfer of funds to these people.”

"Oh, very well." I was by then in an extreme misery of
body and mind. "I do beg your pardon, but I must go
immediately." I rushed gasping from the room and away,
leaving him behind.

IV. Imprisoned

Not only did Cook assist me well with nourishment, she gave me the best of advice in general, having given birth to five healthy children of her own. The doctor called in by Pontsylvania required considerable humoring though I avoided following some of his more awful instructions. What help could purgatives possibly be? There is such a thing as common sense.

I recovered my appetite within a month yet hesitated to reappear in the household at large, at first enjoying the double blessing of feeling well again and relief from Pontsylvania's society. It did not take more than another week, however, for me to know that seven more months confined to my apartments would not be bearable nor would it benefit my constitution in preparation for whatever physical ordeal I must ultimately endure. I also realized, with great sadness, I might be prevented indefinitely from returning to Eisenstein, as my confinement and motherhood could provide Pontsylvania with years of excuses to keep me in Strelsau.

Consequently I determined to emerge from my retirement with a general display of good cheer. I took frequent walks in the garden, saw my dressmakers several times about my maternity wardrobe, ate heartily at dinner, accompanied my husband to the Cathedral for Sunday Mass and went to call on my father.

The Eisen town house in Strelsau was modest by comparison to Pontsylvania House, yet it bore a charm that only the passage of generations can convey upon a fine home. My spirits always lifted when I entered there. We sat out on the terrace in fan-backed willow chairs stuffed with fat flowered cushions, indulging in buttery pastries and strong tea served with hot milk. I announced the news of my condition only to see my dear father fail in pretending to be surprised.

"Oh, Papa, you knew already! Did Gerhard tell you?"

"Actually it was not from Pontsylvania's lips directly that it came to me. It is quite generally known, Hildie." He patted my hand.

"Quite generally known! Before I was given the chance to speak to you?"

"Now Hildie, you can't blame Pontsylvania for being a bit cock-a-hoop about it. I believe he's quite excited, as well he should be."

"And I suppose you've written to Raoul about it, then.

"Hildie! Of course I've not written to Raoul. I'm waiting until after you tell me that you have. So, have you?"

"I have."

"So may I now, then?"

"Oh silly Papa, of course you may." He was a dear old thing, my father. He had never been harsh with me. My eyes filled with tears for a moment.

"Why, Hildie! Are you feeling fragile?"

"No, Papa." I blotted my eyes decisively with my napkin. "I am not feeling at all fragile."

"And your health is entirely good?"

"Absolutely, yes. I feel exceptionally well."

"I am so glad to hear that, as I believe I should be going out to the lands for a time and I wouldn't want to be away from Strelsau if you were having any difficulty. I'd like to consult with young Reynard before the main of the harvest starts coming in. He is capable, remarkably capable, but I must demonstrate my support for his new position of authority. And I must see poor Everard."

"Has Mr. Manx improved at all?"

"I fear not. I am very sorry to say his situation is dire. I am terribly grieved about it; an abominable misfortune never less deserved by any man and although he is in my employ, after all these years together I must say I do count him among my dear friends."

"Oh, Papa! I should go with you."

"Hildie Dear, is that wise?"

"I see no reason why I shouldn't go. In a very comfortable carriage to the train station, of course. Then on to Zenda with you in a private compartment, and another carriage to meet us there."

"Well I'd be glad to have you come, then. Send a note

to inform me when you're ready."

"It shouldn't take me long at all. Two or three days to make a list and pack."

Later that evening, alone in my rooms, I seated myself at my desk and wrote these lines:

Dearest Papa,

Pontsylvania absolutely forbids me to accompany you to Eisenstein. There is no reasoning with him. I am longing to go. I must go. I beg you to intercede with him.

I stared down upon these words for a long time, the pen drying in my hand, my eyes filling with tears for the second time that day. At last I tore the paper to bits, pulled a fresh sheet from a pigeonhole of the desk and began again:

Dearest Papa,

In view of my delicate condition, Gerhard has persuaded me it would be unwise to accompany you to Eisenstein. I know how well you would have enjoyed my company and apologize with all my heart for disappointing you. May God watch over your travels.

With my love as always,
Hilda

Following this painful check by Pontsylvania, I took a leaf from his book for two weeks and avoided him completely. I returned to taking meals in my room, shopped and went for drives accompanied by Elsa or Henriette, made my daily walks on the Grand Mall of Strelsau rather than in the gardens at Pontsylvania House. My husband made no effort to communicate and was probably quite content with the present state of affairs. If there was to be any change, it would be up to me.

There came an evening when I determined to resume at least some pretense of normalcy. I dressed for dinner in a particularly decorative ruched and beaded lavender dress. I powdered my face. I allowed Henriette to fuss more than usual with my hair, sweeping up the whole dark mass of springy curls into a tall formation bound around with narrow velvet ribbons, adding a delicate platinum tiara with five diamond and ruby clusters received as a wedding gift from Pontsylvania's mother, the Dowager Duchess Agathe zu Reinhard and von Plinth.

Early in readiness, I left my apartments immediately after the bell. As I crossed the gallery above the central hall, I heard the opening and closing of a door followed by men's voices. Advancing to the gracefully curved mahogany railing, I looked down to see Pontsylvania traversing the vast marble floor below on his way to the dining room. Accompanying him was Manfred Klench, with whom he was carrying on an animated conversation about the training of hunting dogs. I retreated slowly, sliding my shoes silently over the soft carpet, drawing myself back from their line of sight. Manfred was saying, "But really you must admit, it's not sufficient to employ only rewards with all dogs, especially the bitches which are absolutely always going to be less reliable. If you're going to be in complete control, there must be punishments applied as well."

Sweeping back into my dressing room, I dismissed my maids, then seated myself heavily before the great mirror of my vanity in its ornate frame. With trembling hands, I tore off the tiara and the ribbons. I hung my head, my fingers buried deep in the mass of my ruined hair. *I now reside in hell,* I thought, *condemned for life, God help me.*

It was then, at that very moment of deep and dark despair, that I first felt the movements of my darling child within me.

V. A change of perspective ♛ Conversation with Princess Flavia ♛ Further inroads by Klench

All was transformed as I fully realized my new position at last. I was mother to the heir of the Duchy of Pontsylvania. I knew my power. I moved freely about the house, paying little attention to Pontsylvania. He was diminished in my view and I accepted this with no further sense of disappointment. His approval, or lack thereof, was no longer important to me. The already so beloved life I carried, my child, was everything.

The turning of summer to autumn came with a bracing chill in the air. Pontsylvania and King Rudolph spent more time on their hunts, during which jaunts I felt gloriously free. I ordered the wallpaper and draperies of the breakfast room to be entirely done over in a most improving manner while Pontsylvania was off somewhere in a contest with the King over which of them could shoot a greater number of pheasants. When on his return he predictably complained over what I had done, I suffered a dizzy spell in the midst of the conversation and felt compelled to withdraw. The following morning his mother, the Dowager Duchess Agathe, declaimed upon how delightful the room was and the excellence of my taste, thus creating an awkwardness which could have been no worse had she and I planned it between us though in truth, we did not.

❦ ❦ ❦ ❦ ❦

I received a note of invitation signed by Helga von Strofzin, Lady in Waiting, summoning me to the Royal Palace for Tea with Princess Flavia. A Royal Tea was an occasion I now felt able to approach with far more confidence than before, even when I arrived to find, to my complete surprise, I was the only guest. It was but later I would come to understand some of Flavia's teas were large communal affairs while others would be intimate meetings with ladies in whom she took a personal interest. Having observed me for some time, it was at this point she had determined to draw me a step closer to her inner circle.

She patiently observed my curtsey and then smiled almost impishly as I stood waiting for her to be seated. She said, "I hope you will not mind a chat with me *tête-à-tête*?"

I gazed into her brilliant blue eyes, finding only kindness there. "Your Royal Highness, I am honored. I only hope I may have anything sufficiently interesting to relate."

Her smile grew brighter. "Oh, but I know that you do."

We settled at the table and waited in a companionable silence as an elaborate silver service was rolled in and footed china cups were filled with a steaming brew of perfect color. Platters of tiny sandwiches, sliced fruits and little chocolate cakes were laid between us on a perfectly smooth and spotless white cloth.

"Thank you, Hermann. Thank you, Griselle," said Flavia. "You may leave us." Her servants glided away, silently closing tall gilded double doors behind them.

Flavia promptly poured milk into her tea, stirred it with a tiny silver spoon and took a sip. This was consideration on her part as etiquette required I touch nothing on the table until some food or drink had passed her lips. She said, "I understand, Hilda, you find yourself in a most hopeful condition."

"That is true, Your Highness." I could not help smiling and my smile was comfortably returned.

"While we meet alone here today," she said, "I ask you to address me by my given name. Please do, Hilda. It would please me very much."

To state I was honored would have been redundant, so I simply replied, "I shall. Thank you, Flavia."

"I have suspected," she said, "you've not always been happy these past few months."

There could be no doubt what was meant by this. She referred to my marriage to Pontsylvania. "Happiness is not always a woman's lot," I replied. "Duty is the constant."

"Indeed yes," she said, "You are so right. Yet you are happy now. You have a radiance about you."

"Yes, I am happy. I am filled with joyful anticipation. It's as though the future cannot come soon enough."

"All we woman are doomed to subordination," she said, gazing pensively into her cup. "Regardless of the station to which we are born, we have no charge over our fate. Yet God has granted us the power to be mothers. Can this possibly balance the scales, Hilda? Now that you embark upon it yourself, what is your feeling?"

I had often wondered if Flavia could possibly have a deep affection for Rudolph Elphberg and I now concluded she did not. "I believe it can, Flavia. It has come to me as a complete surprise yet I feel it absolutely to be true."

"Ah, Hilda, you give me great hope." Again she was smiling. "And please do forgive me for asking this question you've no doubt been asked a hundred times: When do you expect the dear one to arrive?

"Sometime in February is is most likely."

"So there will be Christmas to go through and time to spare."

"I shall especially enjoy Christmas this year."

"You may wish to amuse yourself by giving your husband some dreadful gift."

She amazed me with this and she winked, causing me to laugh out loud. I replied, "Why not? His taste is entirely different from mine. Whatever the thing is, he may like it and imagine my aesthetic sense has improved."

"I will be spending Christmastide at home in Gothe-Saxeberg," she said. "For the last time in many years, possibly even the last in my life. It will be bittersweet."

"I also miss my home."

"But did you not grow up here, in Strelsau?"

"I was born in Strelsau but I have not always lived here. My mother loved the life of the city, they say, and didn't want to be anywhere else. She was struck down with brain fever when I was five and we lost her. Then my poor father retreated from Strelsau to our manor house at Eisenstein for years, taking me with him as well as my elder brother, Raoul. The Eisenstein lands are very beautiful and the manor house is spacious and comfortable yet not so formal as a town house. I loved it and I found a dear friend there, Katerina Manx, the daughter of our steward. Kitty is four years older than I. She took me under her care and did all she could to ease the loss of my dear mother. Her own mother had departed to heaven but a year before we took up residence at Eisenstein so there was a deep understanding between us. She was not of my station of course, but my father is such a kind man he did not discourage our closeness, seeing how it comforted me.

"Much of our country there is rugged and wild, with rolling hills, large tracts of fields and woodlands. At the highest point we have our medieval castle, *Schloss* Eisenstein. It's long been a ruin but we'd climb up to it and explore. From our own castle we look out across the river and down upon the one at Zenda. There are both the ancient medieval castle and the chateau completed in 1731. Beyond this, at a greater distance, we can also see the rooftops of the chateau at Tarlenheim. I felt my childhood adventures were as thrilling as any story book. We even had a villain in our story."

"A villain?"

"Well perhaps not literally, but we had a terrible cousin often in residence against whose intrigues we always had to be on guard.

"At Eisenstein I learned things I'd never have been permitted to set my hand to here in Strelsau. Kitty passed on to me whatever she learned herself, including how to cook and all manner of needlework and tailoring. I made some of my own dresses, if you can conceive of such a thing, and they were lovely dresses. And not only did I learn to swim and to ride horseback over rough woodland trails, my brother taught me all about guns: how to take them apart and clean them after they've been fired, which I can tell you is a very dirty business, and how to load and shoot. I possess an elegant pair of parlor pistols he gave me on my sixteenth birthday. To accompany these, the son of our steward crafted me a leather saddle bag with hidden holsters inside, all most beautifully tooled with oak leaves and acorns and my monogram upon a shield. So you see, although you know me now as a duchess and a wife approaching motherhood, in my day I have been nearly so rakish as Rinaldo Rinaldini."

"That does sound like a wonderful life," said Flavia. "Your father was wise to take you away to the country after your tragedy. To lose your mother at such a tender age must have been a terrible sorrow. You spoke of *Schloss* Zenda. So your lands lie close by those of Rudolph's brother, the Grand Duke Michael?"

"Yes, we have a long border with Zenda in the east."

"How interesting; I had not been aware of that. Have

you met the Grand Duke? 'Black Michael,' as I believe he is commonly named?"

"I saw the Grand Duke any number of times, riding by with his huntsmen or in the town, but not when I was old enough to be anyone he'd be introduced to. My father of course does know him yet they've never become close. They're not of the same generation and my father is a scholarly man whose interests tend to be of a different nature."

"And what would you say are the Grand Duke's interests?"

"Well, he's known to be very much a man of the land: riding, hunting, fishing, joining in the harvest. And a champion who exceeds all others at shooting, boxing, fencing and even dancing. Yet they say he finds concerts a bore and has never been to the opera. But Flavia, begging your pardon, are you not yourself well-acquainted with the Grand Duke?"

She bowed her head for a moment. "Hilda, do forgive me. Of course I have met Michael Elphberg on several occasions, the most recent being your own wedding celebration, but all I hear about him comes from the King. I appreciate any opportunity to know what others might have to say. I believe there is some antipathy between Michael and Rudolph which is not openly spoken of, at least not in my company, and which I do not fully understand. I suspect Michael feels a deficiency of esteem for the King and is overly careless in letting it be known."

"This worries you."

She sighed. "Yes. Yes, it does indeed. But these are matters which will not be arranged by women. We can but pray to Our Lord and stand by, or should we have husbands they may listen to us, yet only if they so choose. Now tell me, the Count von Eisen, your father, how did he come to reside in Strelsau again?"

"He brought us back, my brother Raoul and I, when Raoul was sixteen and I was ten, so that Raoul might complete his education here and find his place in society. But we've often returned to Eisenstein ever since, in spring and summer, at harvest time, at Christmas. It will always be home to me."

Sensing all my talk of home had raised a melancholy nostalgia in her heart, I said, "If you wish, Flavia, won't you tell me about how Christmas is celebrated in Gothe-Saxeberg?"

♛ ♛ ♛ ♛ ♛

In the evening, having returned to Pontsylvania House, I chanced to enter the library and found Manfred there alone lounging in a chair before the fire, smoking a thin cigarillo with his cravat loose, his jacket unbuttoned and his booted ankles crossed upon a fine tapestry footstool. He was perusing a book of maps. Displaying his usual impertinent familiarity, he glanced idly at me as I entered, then turned over and folded out another page. I stood silently watching him, my interlaced hands resting upon my newly enlarged frontage. He looked up again, pretended absurdly to have only just noticed me, closed the book and rose to his feet with a studied slowness. "Ah,

38

Hilda. I do beg your pardon. A fascinating book, that."

"Is it really?"

"Well . . . yes. Nothing of any interest to a lady, of course. So Hilda, are you well?"

"Of course, yes. Why wouldn't I be well?"

"Ah." He smirked. "No particular reason I suppose. Just a pleasantry, Hilda."

"Manfred, do you now enjoy free access to this house at any time, or do you come only by invitation?"

His cheeks colored suddenly with a pink stain, his mouth compressed petulantly beneath his drooping moustache. "Of course I am here by invitation."

I smiled with tight lips, my gaze relentless upon his face while the flutter of his black lashes betrayed his nervous blinking. "I've found I am not always informed of the arrangements here in my house. Therefore I simply inquire. Do enjoy your book."

I turned to depart. "Hilda," he said, "Won't you wait a moment?"

I hesitated but did not look back. "What is it?"

"Your condition becomes you, Hilda. You've always been beautiful but never more than now."

"How very kind." I took another step.

He said, "Pontsylvania utterly fails to appreciate his good fortune.

"What?" Still I looked to the door. "Is it possible he complains of me? To you?"

"Oh, Hilda, I would not say that."

"Even if it were true? You men are all in your own

alliance. Good night, Manfred." I passed through the door and closed it decisively behind me, yet not before a swift backward glance revealed him watching me, book hanging in one hand, the small cigar in the other, a speculative expression on his irritating face.

VI. Christmas passes ✤ Arrival of an ally ✤ I inform Pontsylvania of my intentions

I did enjoy Christmas although I missed Raoul even more than usual. Escorted by my father and husband, I attended Christmas Eve Mass at midnight in the National Cathedral of Strelsau. It was a scene of enchantment. The great hanging lanterns and enormous chandeliers, ablaze with thousands of candles, barely pierced the gloom of that vast and lofty space in which hundreds knelt together in prayer. King Rudolph and the Grand Duke Michael appeared side by side in the royal box. They made for a striking comparison. The King tall and fair, his mobile face and restless movements betraying boredom and impatience out of keeping with the grandeur of the occasion. Michael dark, stolid, brooding and undeniably handsome. His bearing was that of a solid military discipline with not a movement wasted. I recalled Flavia's unease over their relationship, yet I foresaw no real danger.

We held a grand dinner and dance at Pontsylvania house on Christmas night, an excellent occasion marred only by the inclusion on the guest list of Manfred and his mother, my Aunt Olympia, who could never speak with me at any length without progressing the conversation to some form of reference to the betrayal of my failure to marry her son. Often she would present these tasteless remarks as jests but I was not amused and I imagine neither was she. I opened the dancing with my husband and then accepted a second dance with my father. Following this display of reasonable effort, I pled my condition and sat out the remainder of the evening, thus denying Manfred any excuse to touch me.

Earlier that day, while we were *en famille* in the grand drawing room and gifts were exchanged around the *tannenbaum*, I had presented Pontsylvania with a watch chain from which depended a crocodile tooth, its gold setting in the shape of a coiled snake with bared fangs and red ruby eyes. He was delighted.

On the first day of the New Year I naturally slept late, finally to be awakened at 11:00 o'clock by Elsa, who said, "Oh Madam, I do so beg your pardon, but there is a girl here and we don't know what to do with her."

I raised myself with some difficulty to a sitting position and reached for the ornate and unreasonably small china cup of chocolate she had placed beside the bed. "What, a caller on such a morning? Surely you could say I'm indisposed and take her card."

"Not a caller, Madam. A common young woman who came to the kitchen door. She carries a letter from you."

I was still befuddled with sleep. "From me?"

"Yes, Madam, from you. Summoning her to come here. She's very anxious to see you. She's been waiting two hours in the kitchen. I can certainly tell her to go away if you wish. Begging your pardon, I was not sure what you would prefer I do, as she does have your letter."

Understanding was coming over me. "Has she brown hair?"

"Yes, Madam, what I would say a chestnut color, in plaits, very long. A nice clean-looking girl she is, though rather too tall."

"Too tall? Is she taller than the Princess Flavia, then?"

"Oh, I'm sure I don't know, Madam."

"Of course you don't know; do forgive me. And now please bring this lady to me at once."

"Oh, Madam, she is not what I would term a lady."

"Well whatever she is, do bring her here immediately."

"But Madam, will you not dress?"

"No, I need not dress. Bring her, please. I also require a pot of chocolate brought, a large one, and another cup, and enough breakfast for two people. No; for three people."

And so within a few moments my dear Kitty was ushered into my presence at last. "Miss Manx, Madam," said Elsa, who then retreated from the room.

Kitty wore a dark brown *dirndl* with a bottle green bodice embroidered with *edelweiss* blossoms, no doubt all of her own making. She performed to me a profound curtsey that would have served for an encounter with royalty. "Your Grace."

"Oh, do stop it," I said. She lifted her fresh and rosy face, revealing a smile.

"Kitty!" I opened my arms and she hastened to embrace me.

"Madam!"

"Oh, please don't call me 'Madam.'"

She drew away and lowered her eyes. "But I must, you know."

"Oh yes, yes; I do understand. But not when we are by ourselves. I have been so lonely here. Please say my name."

"Yes, Madam," she replied gravely, and I knew she was teasing. She looked me up and down. "Oh my, Hilda! Whatever has happened to you?"

"I've grown into a great whale."

"But you look just lovely, Hildie! You are positively glowing."

"Come sit with me!"

She sat on the bed and we embraced again.

"Now you must tell me," I said, "how is your father?"

"Oh, Hildie; he has gone to his eternal rest."

"When was this?"

"A fortnight before Christmas."

"Does my father know?"

"Yes. He came to the church."

"He never told me!"

"He wanted to put it off. He was afraid you'd want to

go to Eisenstein and he worried about your condition. He also said he didn't see the need of spoiling your happiness at Christmas."

"Oh Kitty, I've wanted to see Everard all this time; ever since you wrote to me of his accident. I wanted to go to Eisenstein with Papa. My husband would not allow it. Because of my condition, he claimed, but between you and me, it was his pointless, petty meanness. Oh, I am so sad!"

Elsa entered with the breakfast tray to find Kitty and me both in tears and wrapped in each other's arms. I can't imagine what she thought of this, but she placed the tray swiftly and removed herself, taking pains to be silent in closing the door.

After some time and with several handkerchiefs having been found and employed, Kitty and I resumed our conversation.

"How is Reynard faring?"

"He is well, Hilda, though never have I known him to be so sad as he has become. He is also kept very much occupied with his work, which he says is a great blessing."

"You should return to him soon if he needs you."

"He told me I should go to you. Father's interment will be in May. Perhaps you can be there."

"I intend to be. I will be nursing then, my baby will be quite portable and I shall go to Eisenstein. With you by my side. Here, have a cup of chocolate and you must try these lovely rolls."

"Oh my, yes; thank you; I will. Has it not been good then, Hildie, being a duchess?"

"Not particularly."

"But have you met the King?"

"Three times I believe, though he takes no interest in me nor I in him."

"And the Princess Flavia?"

"Of her I've seen much more and indeed I quite like her but I can hardly see how being known to Princess Flavia will make up for the rest of it all."

In the evening, I found Pontsylvania in the gun room where he was admiring a newly mounted boar's head. "I have a bit of news to relate," I told him.

"What is that?"

"I will be needing a nursemaid shortly. In truth I need one now, to make preparations. I have engaged Katerina Manx."

"Manx? From Eisenstein?"

"Yes."

He looked sternly down his nose at me. "Can this be wise? A common girl from the country while so familiar as well? The choice is bound to raise resentments among the other servants, is is not?"

"Kitty is a charming young woman and will take care to be respectful and helpful to Elsa and Henriette. I'm confident she will put them at ease."

"Can she read or write?"

"Why, of course. At Eisenstein we've always provided for the education of all the children of our tenants and staff, boys and girls alike."

"Have you, indeed?" This was but a rhetorical question, delivered in a dry and faintly contemptuous tone. He turned back to the boar's head. "Doctor Eggismund has given me a list of recommendations. I intended to have the women in and compare their credentials. I really do think I had best proceed with that plan. It is far more sensible."

"Do not waste your time. Gerhard, this is to be a woman into whose hands I must place my baby. I have known Katerina Manx over many years, since I was a little girl. I trust her above any other possible candidate and she is my choice."

"Very well then, if you're going to push me out of this matter I suppose I must accept it. At least for now."

"What is your meaning?"

"I mean the girl may have a trial, but should she not prove satisfactory . . ."

I could not keep myself from staring at the snout of the dead boar with its malignant little glass eyes, the snarling teeth and yellowed tusks, the lolling tongue of dark pink wax. Pontsylvania followed my gaze. "A magnificent fellow, isn't it? I got him with Rudolph's new gun. Too much fire power even for a boar. Dreadful mess it made, but a fine head. A fine head."

VII. Birth of Max ♛ Household intrigues ♛ I further inform Pontsylvania of my intentions

My beloved son, Gerhard Maxim von Plinth, emerged into the world early in the morning on the first day of February. It was an extremely difficult ordeal but with Kitty by my side at every moment, keeping her sharp eyes upon the midwife and Dr. Eggismund, I survived it. The joy that followed suffused everything with such light that even the frequent presence of my delighted husband could not annoy me. It was indeed to be another two months of peace and happiness. Kitty's cheerful and tireless assistance was beyond price and she did endear herself to both Elsa and Henriette, just as I had expected she would.

Late upon an evening in April, there was a tapping at my bedroom door. Kitty, with Max folded in one arm, admitted my husband. He looked down with pleasure at the baby and tickled him under the chin. "How is the dear boy?"

"All is well," I said.

"You will leave us, please, Katerina. No; take the baby with you."

Kitty looked to me with startled eyes. I nodded, and she went out. Pontsylvania closed the door and I felt my heart contract as he turned the key in the lock. He advanced to stand before me and laid his weighty hands upon my shoulders. "You are well, Hilda, are you not?"

"I am well."

"Surely it is time, then, for you to resume that portion of your wifely duty which has been set aside for so long."

"With my apologies, Gerhard, I must decline."

"Decline? You decline? On what basis?"

"There is not sufficient sympathy between us."

"Is there not? I have provided you the means to array yourself in the finest mode and every possible comfort in addition to that fine, healthy baby boy you dote upon. What more does a woman require?"

"It was my duty to provide you with an heir, Gerhard, and I have done so."

"What, a single heir? And if anything should ever happen to the child, what then?"

He had gone too far and I was suddenly stung into a fury. "Why, I should then be obliged to resume my wifely duty. But not at this time. You have vast resources, Gerhard. Surely there is some charming woman in Strelsau, some opera singer or *danseuse*, who would be pleased to comfort you."

He stepped back, his face flushing a fiery red. "Can you possibly mean all these things you say, Hilda?"

"You have shown no interest in mending our relations, Gerhard."

"Mending our relations? What is there to mend, I ask you?"

"Gerhard, the answer to your question is not a simple one. The hour is late and I am too fatigued to commence a lengthy and difficult discussion. If you truly feel an interest in the matter, please speak with me again in the morning and I will sincerely do my best to explain." I stepped swiftly past him, turned the key and threw open the door, thus revealing the faint sound of Max crying in the nursery.

When I emerged from my apartments and went to breakfast the following morning, Pontsylvania was not in the house. Although I would not have imagined this to be so at the time, no further discussion of the problem of our marital relations was destined to occur ever again.

Three days further on, it was Kitty who entered my bedroom and locked the door behind her. She said, "I've found out something."

"Oh, something odious, I suppose."

"Yes. I am sorry, Hilda, but you should know."

"Well, out with it then."

❦ ❦ ❦ ❦ ❦

Three more days passed by. Pontsylvania summoned me to his study, where I found him clipping the end off a fresh cigar over a small chased pewter receptacle which stood on feet appearing to be a set of diminutive hooves. I puzzled over the taxonomy of this unfortunate animal.

"Do sit down, Hilda," he said. He began the noxious process of lighting the cigar. "It has come to my attention, Hilda, you have diverted something on the order of over forty per cent of this month's household budget to a subscription for widows and orphans of common soldiers which is, without a doubt, a mere swindle for gullible women such as yourself. It is unacceptable that you should take it upon yourself to maneuver funds without my knowledge in this way."

"I have not done anything of the kind," I said.

"But I know that you have."

"I have not. I wondered if you would seek to verify it with the bank before accusing me, but I see you did not bother."

He persisted doggedly. "You have done it somehow."

"How do you know this?" His face was obscured in a cloud of smoke. He did not reply. I went on, "I will tell you how you know it, Gerhard. You read about it in my letter I sent to my brother just yesterday. Raoul, unlike yourself, will know it is not true because there is a code word in the paragraph."

The smoke had dispersed to reveal him gaping with dismay. "Code word?"

"Yes. Elsa has been bringing you all my letters so you can open and read them before she replaces the seals and takes them to the post box. Elsa has gone, by the way."

"Gone?"

"Yes. Gone. She is no longer in our employ. No, I did not take it upon myself to discharge her. She has resigned without notice on the grounds that I have spoken to her in an insulting manner, which is perfectly true and nothing that I regret. One hopes she has had the foresight to bank the second salary you've been paying her. I am satisfied, at least for now, Henriette is not another of your secret agents, though I assure you I shall be vigilant. And as we are in this discussion, I have more information for you about my activities; correct information. I shall be taking up residence in the manor house at Eisenstein, indefinitely. Max, Kitty and Henriette will accompany me. Should you wish to see your son, you may visit. You may wish to make use of our hunting lodge, which is quite comfortable.

He pointed the smoldering cigar at my face. "You cannot do this, Hilda; humiliating me like this."

I rose to my feet. "Surely a man of such standing as yourself is above being humiliated by his wife. You may tell your associates whatever you like."

"I will stop your allowance."

"Do so. Only fulfill your obligations to Eisenstein as you have contracted with my father and brother. I will lack for nothing of necessity. I do expect you to provide generously for the needs of your son. As you are a gentleman."

He rose from his chair and leaned towards me, hands spread on the desk. His twisted attempt at a conciliatory smile disgusted me. "Rudolph's coronation is but three weeks away. You bear the duty to make a public appearance in the Cathedral of Strelsau on that day, at my side, as my wife. Hilda, can you not wait?"

I sighed. "Poor Gerhard. You do not understand; perhaps cannot understand; how deeply you have offended me, nor are you sorry. No, I cannot wait. I am going."

VIII. Return to Eisenstein ❧ A skirmish with Klench

Spring at Eisenstein was, for at least a fleeting interlude, as heaven to me. I slept peacefully at night and arose each morning in the spacious tower room where I had passed so many nights of my childhood. I would nurse my sweet Max in a cushioned window seat while gazing out across the greening fields and rooftops of our home farm to the thickly forested slopes beyond. Seen through a cleft in the hills, the frosted line of the Alps drew a jagged horizon at the farthest distance. For a time I could imagine I had never left this place and was not the Duchess of Pontsylvania at all.

As the days grew warmer and the leaves were unfolding, I conceived the notion of an expedition up Wachterberg on horseback.

We set out at mid-morning. It was a crystal clear day with songbirds rioting in the trees. Not counting the baby, there were four in our party: Reynard Manx, Henriette,

55

Kitty and myself. We followed the open road a half mile and then turned off into a narrow trail, at first ascending a gradual slope among wild grasses and brambles. The tiny heads of numerous wildflowers dotted the hillside with sprays of color and the murmuring of thousands of industrious bees could be heard. When at last we slipped under the cool, dark canopy of towering pines, I inhaled the nostalgic scent of their pungent resin and thought of the impossible remoteness of Cairo. There had been five children in residence at the Eisenstein manor house in my time. Three of us were here together now. Manfred was unwanted but Raoul was greatly missed.

It was a slow, lazy ride over a track consisting largely of switchbacks looping back and forth across the steep face of the slope, sometimes within view of each other. As children making the ascent on foot, we had often scrambled up between them. We would clamber over tumbled rocks and fallen trees while cheerfully dirtying our hands, ruining our clothes and getting pitch in our hair.

Reynard rode in the lead. He was the eldest of us, born eight months before Raoul. Unruly corkscrew curls of his ruddy hair bounced beneath the brim of an old felt hat with a pheasant feather in the band. Henriette had requested shyly to go next in line. Reynard rode with a rifle as an ordinary precaution and she stated she was fearful of wild animals. This was not implausible given she was entirely unaccustomed to country life, yet I suspected an additional motive. Whenever the trail widened sufficiently, she would move up beside him and ask questions about our surroundings to which he seemed pleased to respond. She looked elegant riding sidesaddle. Pinned atop her neat blonde coiffure, she wore a green derby with a little spotted bird on the brim. I did feel a pang of jealousy, watching the tilt of their heads, each toward the other, as they conversed. What freedom might it have been, I wondered, to be born a common person without responsibility to the land, the peerage and a great house? I reminded myself the very peak we now ascended and many miles of fine lands surrounding it were ours, the family von Eisen's, and that should be enough.

I rode with two deep baskets hanging before my saddle. In the one at my left were several bottles of cider wrapped up in napkins and a homespun tablecloth. Max was bundled in the one to my right along with accoutrements of infant care, lulled to peaceful slumber by the gentle rocking of the horse. Kitty, at the rear, was in charge of a similar pair of baskets laden with more bottles, buttered bread, cold chicken, cheese, jars of applesauce and spiced cakes.

The final slope we must climb was a set of wide but ruinous moss-covered stone steps. Reynard dismounted and first led my horse up. When I thanked him, he replied "Most welcome, Madam," softening this with a quick direct glance and a certain wry little smile which was typical of him. He went back down to help Henriette while Kitty fended for herself with all capability.

The steps had brought us to a broad causeway across which we approached a wide gap in a wall of stone blocks rising to a towering height. The ruin of a massive oak and iron portcullis had long since fallen for the final time. Off to one side was the arched opening of what had been a postern gate, wide and high enough to comfortably admit a horse and rider. Entering this dark and rather forbidding portal, we processed in single file through a tunnel of about twelve feet in length to emerge again into sunlight in the inner courtyard of *Schloss* Eisenstein. We all dismounted, tethering our horses to parts of the old portcullis. Reynard carefully detached and lifted down the basket in which Max slept, passing it to me and Kitty, who would carry it slung between us. We all crossed to the parapet to admire the view. Henriette, having never been there before, exclaimed aloud in wonder and delight.

The side of Wachterberg we had just ascended was steep enough, but the opposite side was an almost sheer drop to the river. Upon our left, a mile upstream, could be seen the great falls of Weisspferde. Even at this distance, the constant roar of the waters could be faintly heard. Also to our left, and so close as to be almost beneath us, was the fall known as the Little Sister, shooting a narrow stream outward and then down a long drop into a circular basin carved into the rock over centuries by the rotating action of the water. From this natural vessel, another fall coursed through a smooth notch in the stone and dropped to the surface of the river.

Off to our right, at the bottom of the valley and on the opposite bank, was the seat of the Grand Duke Michael of Strelsau at Zenda. The ancient castle there was contemporary with ours, but the Eisenstein castle had been a watchpost while Zenda's was a fortress of major size now flanked by a great 18th century chateau. The old castle had towers at its four corners as well as a large block-shaped central keep. It stood upon a natural island of rock within a broad moat supplied by the river. A drawbridge supported by stone pylons spanned from the outer gate of the castle to a circular drive; this in turn connecting with an avenue lined with poplars, sweeping up to the stately columned portico of the chateau. A complex of stables, barns and other structures sprawled out behind that great mansion. From our lofty vantage point, it was as if looking down over a toy scene from a fairy tale. Threads of smoke rose from the chimneys and a seemingly tiny banner fluttered bravely in the wind. Several miles beyond, in a fold in the hills, could also be seen the red tiled rooftops, chimney pots and conical towers of the chateau at Tarlenheim. As we looked down, six dark specks emerged from behind the chateau of Zenda, moving in formation along the drive and then out to the roadway. These were men on horseback riding at great speed. They soon disappeared over the horizon, heading south.

In the center of the courtyard of our castle stood a well head with a massive iron-bound oaken cover fully six feet wide. I had always had a bit of a horror of this well. According to local lore, it connected to an underground watercourse which ran deep beneath Wachterberg. The original well shaft long predated the castle in its final form, which had been built up around it over several generations of the tribal barons of antiquity. When we were children, we had shifted the cover slightly with great efforts and dropped pebbles in to discover how long it would take for them to make a sound, only to find we could hear nothing at all until Raoul managed to force through a rock the size of a man's head. As we held our breaths to listen, this produced a receding series of faint sounds as it bounced off the walls of the shaft, yet still no final splash or impact could we discern. There were tales of human skeletons from medieval times down in the bottom of the well, including one dark local legend, the veracity of which I have never ascertained, of a man chained up and thrown in alive as punishment for some act of treachery. Raoul was not fearful of ghosts and likely would have enjoyed seeing one but I wasn't quite so cool about the subject. As an impressionable little girl, I had suffered nightmares about that well.

The surface of the well cover stood waist high and would serve as a table on which to lay out our provisions as it had done many times in the past. I made up a baby's nest from a blanket on the shady side of it while Kitty and Henriette set about transferring and unpacking baskets. Reynard knelt beside me holding the one in which Max still slept. There was a sudden lift of his head as something caught his eye. He said, "Mr. Klench is here."

Rising quickly to my feet, I saw that indeed this was unfortunately true. Manfred was approaching briskly across the stone pavement of the courtyard, hat in hand, the breeze lifting tendrils of his black hair. Ignoring the presence of Kitty, Henriette and Reynard, he bowed to me.

"Hilda! How pleased I am to find you. May we have a word?"

"Did you follow me here all the way from Strelsau?" I asked.

"Why no, of course not, Hilda. I've come out to see my mother as I often do."

"Aunt Olympia is at the house."

"Indeed," he said. "I have just been there with her. But now, as we are both here . . ." He offered his arm.

It would have been Aunt Olympia who had informed him as to where he could find me. I did take his arm and walked with him to the far side of the watch tower which stood close by the parapet, resolving to make quick work of our conversation. We stood in the wind and faced each other. He waved an expansive arm in indication of the spectacular view surrounding us. "Grand to return to the old place, is it not?"

"Yes. It is good to be here." I could not resist a glance upward as I recalled how a ten year-old Manfred, in a rage at Raoul over some affront the nature of which I could no longer remember, had carried his tiny white curly-haired dog, Fritzi, up nearly to the top of the tower we now stood beside and either pushed or driven her out through a loophole. Of course he had not let anyone actually see him do it but Fritzi was so tiny and the steps so steep, a voluntary climb would have taken great effort without any imaginable motive, nor was she a suicidal dog, nor had she been alone in the tower. I, myself had spied Manfred slipping out shortly after her fall with what appeared to me as a demeanor of smug self-satisfaction from head to toe. Fritzi had broken her back on the stones of the courtyard. Raoul lay down beside her for an hour until one of our gamekeepers arrived and mercifully shot her. There had followed a miserable scene at home presided over by my father and Aunt Olympia, with Raoul in a black, stony silence and the accused Manfred weeping while outrageously claiming Fritzi had climbed the tower and gone out through the loophole of her own volition while he, rather than calling out to warn Raoul of the dog's sudden attack of inexplicable self-destructive insanity, had taken it upon himself alone to follow her up and attempt to quietly cajole her into his rescuing hands. That was perhaps the most incredible aspect of all to his story, that he would have gone to the effort of climbing up a dirty old tower, physically exerting himself, breathing hard, perhaps even sweating, maybe scuffing a shoe or getting a cobweb in his hair, all out of concern for Raoul's dog. To those of us who really knew him this was impossible to believe. He had been sent away for three months while we were urged to consider our own parts in the chain of events leading up to Fritzi's demise and to seek forgiveness in our hearts. Three months no doubt gave Raoul and Reynard plenty of time to plot some inevitable act of retribution, though what form that took was a secret I was never privy to.

"So, Hilda," Manfred declared, failing to conceal a note of triumph, "You have left Pontsylvania."

"Oh, nonsense. I can't think who you have been listening to. I have not 'left' anything. I am visiting my home."

"He says you have. Left him, that is. He said it to me."

"Really? If he did in truth speak those words, he was surely being overly dramatic as well as indiscreet."

Manfred grasped me by the elbow, bending toward my ear with an eagerness that made me wish to recoil, though I held quite still. His voice dropped to a confidential tone. "You should break with him, Hilda. I can help you. I know many things about him. I can obtain proofs."

"Oh good Heavens, Manfred! What a fine and loyal friend Gerhard has in you, I must say."

"My dearest cousin Hilda is far, far more important to me than my friend Pontsylvania. As she has always been, and always will be."

"Gerhard is the father of my son, Manfred. I have no intentions in the direction you suggest."

"You will change your mind, Hilda, once you hear all that I have to tell you."

I was losing my temper and my voice began to rise. "I have no wish to hear it!"

"But you will be making a tremendous mistake, Hilda, if you do not."

"Well I shall make a tremendous mistake, then."

"Come now, Dear Hilda. You cannot possibly be happy living with Pontsylvania and who could blame you? Neither his title nor his bloated bank account can make him even remotely worthy of you. The man is an ass. You know it. Everyone knows it. You owe it to yourself to consider what I have come to offer you."

"Manfred, you must stop."

He was drawing me closer. I began to resist and the clutch of his insistent fingers hurt my arm. "Please, I do beg of you, if you will but hear me out, Hilda!"

"I am telling you, Manfred, I am not interested in what you have to say about Gerhard and I will not hear it."

"There is a woman, Hilda . . . "

"Oh, Manfred, for shame; let go of me now and do stop!"

To my surprise Reynard suddenly appeared, looming over Manfred's shoulder with the still-drowsing Max cradled in his arms. "Begging your pardon, Mr. Klench," he said.

Manfred rounded on him, hissing an oath under his breath. "What do you WANT, Manx?"

"It's about your horse, Sir. She has got loose."

"That is impossible!"

"It must be possible, Sir, as I've just seen her halfway down the steps. She looked to be heading back to the trail."

Manfred had gone red in the face. "Why then did you not stop her, you stupid buffoon?"

Reynard took a step back and looked down upon Max who was yawning in his arms, throwing out his chubby fists. "Again begging your pardon, Sir, I could not chase your horse as I was holding this baby."

"Well then give the damn baby to one of these women and get after the horse!"

Reynard's blue glance swiftly met my eyes and dropped away.

"No," I said.

Manfred turned back to me. "What?"

"I said no. Mr. Manx is in my employ and he is going to continue to assist me here and not go off in pursuit of your horse that you have failed to tie up properly. I do also enjoin you never again to curse in reference to my child. I will see you later at the house, assuming you succeed in making your way back there."

Manfred's complexion had altered from its initial flush to a sickly paleness, especially about the mouth. He turned again to Reynard and hissed between his teeth, "You have done this, Manx!"

Reynard returned his gaze with a placidly blank expression. "I am very sorry to know, Sir, you consider me capable of such a thing."

Manfred jammed his hat back onto his head. "I will see you again, Manx."

"Naturally, Sir, one certainly hopes for that."

Manfred walked swiftly toward the postern. I could sense he wanted to run but would not so sacrifice his dignity within our sight. He went out. Reynard gently handed Max into my arms. As our heads leaned close together, he murmured, "I hope I have not done wrong."

"You have not done wrong," I replied, "but he will not forget. You will have to be on your guard."

"With Mr. Klench, Madam, to be on guard is a perpetual state of affairs so I shall just go on as usual."

I sighed. "I expect I shall be required to look at him over the dinner table this evening while making polite conversation."

"Perhaps not. I believe it's today Madame Klench plans to travel back with him to Strelsau so they may attend the coronation of King Rudolph."

"Oh, the coronation. I had quite forgotten."

"It is tomorrow."

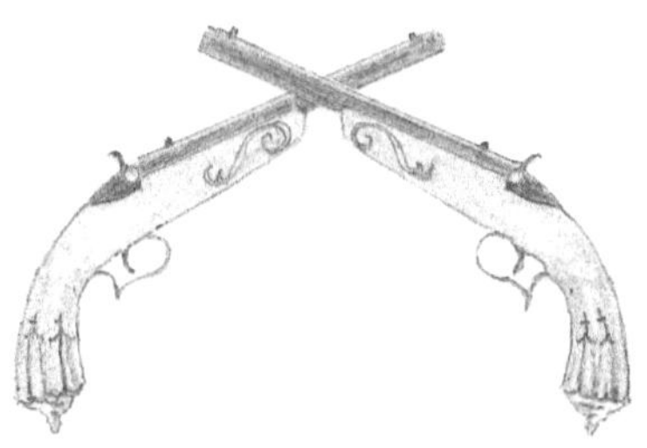

IX. A strange encounter ❧ A conversation with Reynard

I went out riding the following morning early while the dew still beaded the grass and a drifting mist hovered over the surface of the river. I rode south, letting the horse out at a gallop all the way down to the bridge that crosses to the village of Zenda. After turning back in the direction of home, I entered a familiar opening through the hedgerow leading into a well-worn path. This track brought me down to a brook with a pool where I could let my horse dip in for a brief drink.

As I was passing out again through the hedge, a man's voice shouted "Ah-hah, Antoinette!" and I was startled indeed to find myself immediately beside another horse upon my left, the rider of which had seized my own by the bridle. I was brought up to an abrupt halt and was so close against him, my knee pressed into his leg. He was laughing uproariously.

He was a finely dressed gentleman and a complete

stranger to me. On the hand restraining my horse, I noted a gold ring bearing a great square ruby. I drew a pistol from its hidden sheath within my saddle bag while simultaneously cocking the hammer, a quick maneuver I had practiced to perfection years before. I pressed the barrel to his shoulder. His laughter instantly ceased and his dark eyes widened in surprise. He released my horse and backed his own out into the roadway, where he stopped. I noted his mount to be a magnificent coal black steed, its bridle and stirrup leathers adorned with trappings of chased silver. I aimed the pistol at his knee.

There was a moment of breathless silence as we simply stared at one another. Then his mouth drew into a broad grin, flashing white teeth beneath a small moustache trained to sharp points. To my puzzlement and irritation, he tossed back his head and resumed laughing.

I said, "Pray do amuse yourself elsewhere."

He swept off his hat, revealing a tumble of loose dark curls. "Madame, I must abjectly beg your pardon. You are so well disguised under that great boat of a *chapeau* you've bound to your head, I mistook you for a completely different exquisitely lovely lady."

"You stand in a close relation with that lady, evidently."

"I should certainly wish to." His gaze wandered from my face down to my boots and back again. "But I must apologize once more, for I believe I have addressed you incorrectly. Your Grace, is it not? One so elegantly mounted and arrayed as you, found riding in this location, so lovely and yet not the very lovely lady I had imagined her to be, could only be Eisenstein's celebrated Duchess."

"I need not identify myself to you, Sir."

He leaned forward over the horse's neck, his hat dangling negligently from his fingers. His coat was open, revealing a wine red brocade vest and beautifully wrought gold watch chain. He was a young man, remarkably handsome with his long, tousled curls and eyes fringed with black lashes. His smile was undeniably appealing yet I sensed a faint, disquieting hint of avarice. He indicated the pistol with a glance and a lift of his chin. "That's a pretty toy you have there. Would you truly shoot my poor horse?"

In answer, I raised my aim to the top of his thigh. He backed his horse a few more steps. "Ah, well, this a peculiar first meeting," he said, "but it need not be our last. One hopes we shall soon be properly introduced in polite society. Then perhaps we can enjoy a dance together rather than you shooting me." He held his hat to his chest and bowed. "That you may recall me then, I take the liberty of saying I am Rupert von Hentzau."

"You are a gentleman, then."

He inclined his head in assent. "Such is the fortune of my birth."

"It has always been my understanding a gentleman will never remain where he is not wanted."

Again he was laughing. "*Touché*, Your Grace! *Adieu*, and I look forward to our next encounter." He wheeled his horse, replaced his hat and dashed off up the road. I watched him, resting the weight of the pistol upon my saddle, until he crossed to Zenda. Halfway over the bridge he halted to look back in my direction. Seeing me still there, he flamboyantly waved his hat. Then his horse leaped forward at a gallop and he shortly vanished from my sight.

As I rode homeward, I glimpsed him once again through the trees on the far side of the river, still riding full out, flying up the road that followed the opposite bank toward the chateau of Michael, Grand Duke of Strelsau.

♛ ♛ ♛ ♛ ♛

That evening, I tapped at the door and entered the room we had always named as the back parlor. This was part of the Manx family's apartments within the rear annex of the house, but any of us would often be invited in. I had always loved this room as it was so comfortable yet quite informal and unpretentious. It had been the scene of many a boisterous game of cards, the roasting of chestnuts in a pan on the grate, the tying of pine garlands at Christmas and more such convivial activities fondly recalled.

Reynard was seated behind a table by the window, a pair of brass lamps illuminating his work. He rose as I entered, a pen in his hand. "Your Grace."

"Oh please, call me 'Hilda' while we're here in this old familiar place."

"Yes, Madam," he said with his small, wry smile.

"And do sit."

"Thank you."

Two armchairs with embroidered cushions stood at

either end of a worn velvet settee before the fireplace, where a small blaze burned against the evening chill. I settled into one of these.

"I see you are occupied," I said. "I'll not distract you for long."

"I am nearly finished. Stay as long as you like."

"The day's accounts?"

"Yes."

"Does all go well?"

"Exceedingly well. A dozen more lambs birthed this week and three calves."

"Oh, I should like to see the lambs."

"Well you must see them, then. Notwithstanding the fact that life is short and some of them will soon be eaten."

"And some not?"

Smiling, he replied, "Yes, some not, though those must instead grow into shaggy obstreperous beasts with devil's eyes."

"They are endearing little creatures."

"They are, yet in my opinion there is nothing more endearing in all the animal kingdom than a piglet. We shall have piglets in a week or two."

"Well I must see the piglets as well, then." There was a fat tabby cat stretched out on the hearth rug. I asked, "Can this be Muffin?"

"It is she. Muffin lives yet. We have a number of her offspring about as well and indeed they are scattered throughout the households of Eisenstein. We try our best to limit her procreational activities but every two or three years she will outwit us. I never could bring myself to drown kittens, nor will I assign that task to another. One of my weaknesses."

"I could not do it either," I said. I bent down to stroke the cat. She rolled ecstatically onto her back, offering up her rotund, spotted tummy.

"There, look," said Reynard, "She remembers you well."

"You remind me of your father, sitting there like that."

"Oh, he is sitting here still. At my elbow, endeavoring to stop my mistakes."

"If you will forgive me, what happened to him, Reynard? How did he come to fall?"

"We will never know. He'd been knocked about the head and was insensible when he was found. After he finally came awake again, he could never remember what had taken place, only riding alone beforehand on his way back from a visit at the Braun cottage. Something must have startled the horse into a terror, for he'd been knocked or thrown off and then dragged for some distance."

"Oh! Dear God."

"Indeed last year and its subsequent winter has been the most sorrowful time of my life, though now with the spring it begins to ease a bit."

"Reynard, I am so very sorry."

"His remains are to be finally lowered in the churchyard in two weeks time." Elbows on the table, he passed his hands up his clean-shaven cheeks and smoothed the unruly red curls back from his high, fair forehead. "I rather dread it, but it must be got over."

"I will be there."

"I'm glad of that, Hilda."

This was the first time he had spoken my given name since I had arrived. I would not draw attention to it, but secretly it pleased me.

"I wanted to ask you," I said, "about a person I saw this morning. While I was out riding I encountered a strange young man on the road."

"Did he give a name?"

"Hentzau."

"Rupert von Hentzau?"

"Yes."

"Did he know who you were?"

"I did not say, but he guessed."

"He was insolent to you, then?"

"Yes, rather."

"Yet charming at the same time."

"I see you do know him."

"I know the man. He is counted among Black Michael's most intimate circle of friends. It was due in part to his frequent presence in and around Zenda I urged Kitty to go to you in Strelsau as soon as our father passed away. He had taken notice of her, you see."

"Taken notice?"

"Yes. He does not confine his attentions to ladies of his own class."

"But surely Kitty is astute enough not to be taken advantage of."

"Indeed she is. My fear was that at some time he might come upon her alone in an opportunely remote setting and then she would be given no choice."

"No choice?"

"It is said he has done such things before. I mark him to be a very dangerous man. He has great charm, as you have seen, and he is admired by both women and men. He is physically courageous. He does well at whatever he attempts. He can shoot, run, climb, swim; he's accomplished at fencing, a good dancer . . .

"He sounds rather like the Grand Duke Michael himself, then."

"They do have much in common. But Hentzau is one of a certain type of man who can be found among every class from molecatchers to kings. He is a hunter."

"A hunter?"

"Yes, a hunter. He lives for the chase, the enjoyment of a challenging pursuit for its own sake. Once he is fixed upon some object of desire, he will go relentlessly on to any length to attain it. Then, having made his capture, he will soon discover a fresh objective. Had he been born a prince, there would be perpetual war. If he were a cottager's son, he would be a formidable poacher. As it is, his pursuits are the advancement of his fortune and his *amours*."

There followed a silence during which he gazed down at his open account book with unseeing eyes. "If you will forgive me, Madam, perhaps you should not ride alone. I can assign a good man to accompany you."

"I would rather it were yourself, Reynard, if your

duties will allow for it."

"Of course, if that is what you wish."

"Tomorrow then, if the weather is fine, let us ride out to look at the lambs."

"Certainly." He had been still staring down at the ledger, pondering. He lifted his clear blue eyes to meet mine. "In what direction was Hentzau going?"

"North, toward the chateau of Black Michael."

"It is extremely odd, don't you think? That Hentzau should have been where you saw him this morning rather than in Strelsau where King Rudolph's coronation was about to take place? I wouldn't have thought such an ambitious fellow would miss that occasion for anything."

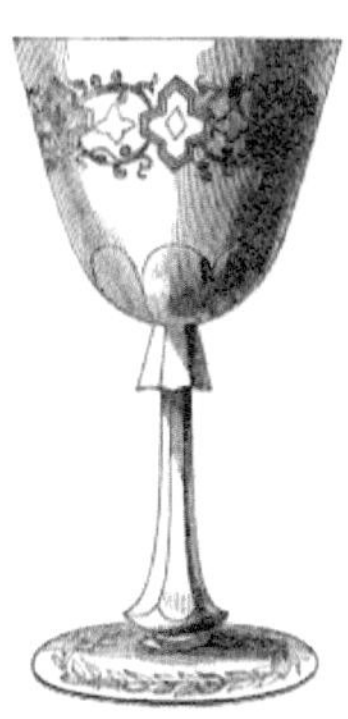

X. Pontsylvania visits Eisenstein, to his peril

The days passed in peace at Eisenstein. There were lambs and there were piglets. Aunt Olympia returned from her attendance at the coronation escorted not by Manfred, but by my father, who stayed with us for a fortnight during which the solemn interment of the remains of Everard Manx took place. Then shortly after his departure for Strelsau there was a barn fire at one of the cottages, a pitched battle fought all night under Reynard's calm and tireless direction. No lives were lost, human or animal. Max began to get a tooth.

Eventually a letter arrived from Pontsylvania:

My Dear Hilda,

I trust you have been enjoying your respite from the strains of life in Strelsau. As you previously suggested, I propose to bring a small hunting party to the lodge at Eisenstein. I am inclined to a leisurely holiday and will travel by the roads. I would expect to arrive alone at some time on the 21st inst. with two or three gentlemen to join me the following day or perhaps later. I look forward to calling on you and our dear boy. I would hope we may have some discussion of your eventual return to Pontsylvania House, where you are greatly missed. If you will confirm the date, I will write to Mr. Manx about my requirements.

 Yours sincerely,
 GRvP

I had known I would have to see him sooner or later. I posted a short note confirming the date.

Not long thereafter as we we were out riding early one morning, Reynard said to me, "I have a letter from His Grace, your husband. He requests I meet him at the hunting lodge on the 21st which will be this Tuesday next. He asks me to bring a few provisions and help him to find his way around the wine cellar, and he wants to discuss his plans. He says he'll require no cook or other staff until the following day and won't want a gamekeeper until the day after that."

"Very well, then," I said. "I do appreciate your assistance in this and that you keep me informed." I wanted also to say I was terribly sorry for the imposition, but that would have been improper. I could not see why Pontsylvania needed to so involve the steward of our estate in his recreational pursuits, yet it was not really surprising given his inflated sense of his own importance.

That Tuesday night of the 21st, I lay awake very late anticipating Pontsylvania might appear on our doorstep as soon as the coming morning and dreading the encounter. I attempted to picture him in the Eisenstein hunting lodge, a part of my family's holdings he had never previously invaded, engaged there in a discussion with Reynard of his plans to entertain his gentleman friends. This quite defied my imagination. I fell asleep at last, but not for long.

Kitty was sitting on the edge of the bed and shaking me by the shoulders. "Hilda! Hilda, wake up! Hilda!"

"I am awake." Drawing myself up to prop my back against the carved oaken headboard, I perceived the twin lamps at either end of the mantlepiece were alight: also that Kitty was fully dressed in blouse, bodice and riding skirt, yet her loose hair hung down over her hips and her feet were bare. "What time is it?"

"I don't know: past midnight surely. You must see Reynard."

"Reynard? He has come back from the lodge?"

"Yes."

"Kitty, what is happening?"

"You must see Reynard this instant." She went to the door, which stood slightly ajar, and to my astonishment, drew Reynard by the arm into the room and shut the latch behind him.

Reynard brought into my bedroom in the middle of the night? What could this mean? I was about to demand the explanation but as he stepped into the light and I saw his face, the words died on my lips. He came to my bedside and fell to his knees. "Your Grace, I do not know where to begin. Oh Madam, I am so terribly sorry."

"Why? What has happened?"

"It is your husband. Oh, how can I tell you?"

I was struck with a terrible dread and my heart turned so cold within me, I felt it could scarce continue beating. "Just speak it."

Reynard's head, already bowed, hung lower. "He is dead. His Grace the Duke, your husband, is dead."

"Dead! Dead? Are you sure of this?"

"Absolutely certain, of course, or I should never, ever say it to you. He is dead."

"But how?"

"He lies on his bed in the hunting lodge. I believe he has been poisoned."

"Poisoned! God in Heaven! What can possibly have poisoned him?"

"If you could see his eyes . . . It is belladonna, or something like it."

"But how could such a thing have happened?"

"It is not so much how, Madam, as who. Manfred von Eisen Klench has done this thing. To your husband and to me."

"Klench! Manfred is at the lodge?"

"He is not at the lodge. He was there but now has gone, leaving behind no trace of himself as if he were never there at all. Leaving me alone with the Duke murdered and the hangman's noose around my neck. Before God, though I remain alive tonight I do believe we'll soon find your cousin has both disgraced and killed me."

I drew the bedcovers close around me, for I was

shivering with shock. "Please," I said. "Get up off your knees and sit. Tell me everything as it happened."

Kitty was on a chair by the fireplace, hastily stuffing her feet into a pair of boots. "Tell it quickly," she said. "We have to decide what it is we're going to do."

Reynard drew a footstool closer to the bed and seating himself upon it, buried his ashen face in his hands.

Kitty began hastily winding and pinning her hair, having ready across her lap a scarf to tie around her head. "Tell her, Reynard. Get on with it."

Reynard lifted his face, steeling himself. Gazing directly into my eyes and without further hesitation, he gave this account: "I went to meet His Grace the Duke as he had requested in his letter, bringing with me a ham and some bread and butter and a few other such things. Your cousin Mr. Klench was there with him. His Grace stated they were very hungry and would sit down at table straight away but he would wish to speak with me afterwards. He directed me to bring a number of bottles up from the cellar and pull the corks. I did that and left the room until after some time had passed, when Mr. Klench called out and invited me in a most jovial manner to join them in a toast. They had been drinking wine with their supper but the toast was to be drunk from a set of tall cordial glasses with *schnapps*, a new bottle of which I opened while they watched. I stood with them and Mr. Klench made a series of toasts. To the newly crowned King. To the Princess Flavia. To the Grand Duke Michael. To Pontsylvania. To Eisenstein. And to you, Madam. I did notice he re-filled my glass and that of the Duke to the very rim each time yet his own he was filling but half full; I took this to be a sort of ordinary gentlemen's pranking disguised as generosity. After all this I retired to the service room off the pantry to wait until I was wanted. They were very merry over supper and their drinking. Mr. Klench was relating long anecdotes of the sort gentlemen do not tell in mixed company, one after another, and they were laughing a great deal. After hearing this go on for some time I came to the conclusion I was likely to be kept waiting all night and I had felt compelled to drink an excessive amount of *schnapps* in a very short time, so I lay down across a row of chairs and began to doze off. Mr. Klench then came to find me, saying he required immediate assistance with the Duke, who was much the worse for drink and must be helped to bed. We found His Grace still seated with his head down on the table. He spoke as we lifted him up between us but he could not stand and his words were so run together, I could make nothing of what he was trying to say. We walked him, or indeed fairly dragged him on his feet, to his room and got him laid out on the bed. He clutched my sleeve and continued to talk and seemed rather excited about something but still I could not understand him. I started to light the lamp on the night stand but Mr. Klench instructed me not to take the trouble. He loosened the Duke's cravat and covered him with a blanket while I pulled his boots off. His Grace went suddenly off to sleep and began snoring. Mr. Klench then dismissed me rather abruptly, saying he would be going straight to bed himself and nothing further was required of me. He did state he appreciated my assistance very much, which struck me as odd, coming from him. Indeed his demeanor the whole evening had been odd. He had paid me attention in such an uncharacteristic manner, while usually he most pointedly ignores me, and so I felt suspicious while having no knowledge of what to suspect. He bade me get back to sleep, saying the Duke would surely expect my presence first thing in the morning, that he might give the instructions he had failed yet to impart. I returned to the service room. Having been roused once had made me all the more groggy and I fell into a heavy sleep for well over an hour before something woke me again. I don't know what it was; perhaps that my surroundings had not been absolutely silent before yet suddenly that was so. I was feeling all the more uneasy. I rose and lit a candle and walked about in my stocking feet. I recalled how loudly His Grace the Duke had been snoring yet I could hear nothing. I went to stand in the doorway of his room and listened. I could not hear him breathing. I stepped in and touched him and found that he was dead. I lit the lamp by the bedside so as to get a better look at him. His eyes . . . Despite that he had been certainly asleep when I left him, his eyes were open and the pupils were so wide and black, the irises had disappeared. Until then I had been struggling against the influence of the *schnapps*, but in those few moments I was shocked stone sober. I shouted out for Mr. Klench and went to what was to have been his room. He was not there. The bed had not been slept in and there was nothing of his in the room. I thought I must have mistaken his room so I hastened to look into all the other rooms, finding no signs of occupation. Then despite that I was without my boots I ran out to the stable. I found that Mr. Klench's horse, guns and other equipment had been entirely removed. Returning into the great room, I saw also that his plate, cutlery and glasses were no longer on the table. Only His Grace the Duke's things remained as if he had sat there eating and drinking by himself. One wine glass was half full with a single open bottle beside it. All the other bottles had disappeared. I went back to where I had been sleeping to retrieve my coat and boots. The coat I found to be reeking of peppermint and the *schnapps* bottle, completely emptied, lay on the floor. I expect Mr. Klench will appear tomorrow to meet the other gentlemen of the hunting party and will say nothing of having been at the lodge tonight. Madam Baeder is to cook for them and plans to go over with an assistant first thing in the morning. His Grace had set down in writing his instructions that I should meet him at the lodge. It is known that I went to do so and remained away from here long after all had gone to bed. It is also known I meant to carry provisions to the lodge and those will be found there. There will be no sign of Mr. Klench having accompanied the Duke and if I claim it he will say I lie and that I bear some grudge against him. I have to think His Grace the Duke's decision to summon me there alone was somehow due to his infuence or direction."

"That is perfectly credible," I said, "for he has wrapped my husband around his little finger and rendered him entirely suggestible by means of flattery and false camaraderie. I believe the Duke to have become convinced Manfred is the best and wisest of all his friends.”

“I fear Mr. Klench will make some testimony, perhaps provide some point of evidence, to demonstrate why I would wish to harm the Duke. I can only wonder what it may be.”

Kitty, who had not been idle during this narrative, was throwing a set of my riding clothes onto the bed. “You are a fool if you don’t know what it will be. It will be about Hilda! Always it is about Hilda. The man is obsessed.” She was hissing in a loud whisper. If not for knowing Max was asleep in my dressing room, she might have been shouting. She turned to me. “Do you not see? He kills two birds with one stone. He actually imagines with your husband out of the way, he will get you to marry him yet. Indeed he means to make a hero of himself, being the man to bring the murderer of the Duke to justice, and thus he will have his final revenge upon Reynard, which he has no doubt been stewing over since his embarrassment that day up on Wachterberg.”

“But what with regard to me could suggest Reynard would have cause to poison my husband?”

“Perhaps,” Kitty replied, “That you and my brother have fallen into a habit of going riding together nearly every morning.”

“But Manfred does not know that.”

“Oh, yes he does. He knows all that goes on here. Since you arrived, his mother has been posting him so many letters she rarely misses a day. Hilda, we must do something!”

"Indeed we must." I threw off the covers and put my feet out of the bed.

Reynard rose in haste, turning his back so as not to look upon me in my nightdress. "What can you possibly do?"

"I don't quite know yet. I shall have to go and see."

"I must come with you."

"Certainly not. You cannot return to the lodge."

"But, Madam!"

"Reynard, I absolutely forbid it. You are out of this. We will not play into Manfred's hand."

"How then may I help you?"

"Stay right here and watch over Max until we return. Do this for me, Reynard. The horse you rode back from the lodge. Is it still saddled?"

"Yes."

"A few minutes saved, then."

"I will wait out on the landing while you dress." He moved to the door but then stopped for a moment with a slight turn of his head in my direction. "You do believe me, Hilda? You can believe me? That I did not harm your husband, and that Mr. Klench was there?"

"Of course I believe you. My Cousin Manfred is like none other. It is some congenital sickness of the mind and a terrible curse upon the family von Eisen, God help us."

XI. At the hunting lodge
in the small hours

Kitty and I set forth without lights. It was an overcast night but a gibbous moon behind the clouds afforded the faint illumination required to keep to the road, sometimes at a trotting pace, sometimes a canter. The chirping of the multitude of crickets in the hedgerows was no louder, it seemed to me, than the pounding of my heart. The distance we must travel, though not long, felt interminable. I even suffered an irrational moment of fear we had somehow missed our destination in the dark, but then we came to it.

Leaving the roadway, we passed between two great square gateposts of moss-encrusted stone. We were in a lane that entered the woods a half mile north of the entrance to the Wachterberg trail. The gloom was so deep beneath the trees, we had to dismount there and lead the horses. We had brought a dark lantern from the Eisenstein stable, an item of equipment sometimes used by our gamekeeper when stalking poachers. Kitty proceeded to kindle this. She opened a shutter and a narrow shaft of light appeared, projecting downward upon the ground.

The Eisenstein hunting lodge had been constructed in the 1790s at the behest of the Countess Maria zu Bauer and von Eisen, who desired an end to gangs of hunting gentlemen continually occupying her house, as well as alternate walls and floors on which to display the many heads, masks, horns and skins of the victims of their sport. It was a hostel of generous size consisting of a single story built of field stone with pine paneling in the interior. Within was a spacious great room behind which a series of private bedrooms opened out of a single long corridor. In later years, a large wood-shingled addition had been built on to house a pantry and rooms to accommodate the gentlemen's attendants, who originally had done all their cooking out of doors and slept in the stables. There were a number of outbuildings: stabling for horses, carriages and wagons as well as a large butchering shed, storage sheds, and so forth.

We did not tether our horses outside but brought them into the stable. Pontsylvania's favorite hunter, Sophie, was in a box there alone. His saddle, bridle and favorite rifle we found there also, neatly placed together. From the stable yard, we then followed the beam of the dark lantern along a stone paved walkway leading to the service entrance of the lodge. This was a broad, iron-bound oaken door. I opened it while Kitty stood by, and the loud snap of the latch startled me despite that my own thumb had pressed the lever. We stepped into a square passage where pairs of worn wooden sabots and heavy leather boots stood in an orderly line against the wall to our right. From cloaks and coats on a row of hooks above them, there came the distinctive and vaguely unpleasant odor of oilskins.

Kitty opened another shutter of the dark lantern, sending forth a second beam of light projecting straight ahead. We passed on into the pantry, where we found the ruins of a ham and a dish of butter, the end of one loaf and another uncut, a crock of mustard, a jar of pickles standing open, a hunk of cheese wrapped in oiled paper. The empty *schnapps* bottle stood there also where Reynard, having previously retrieved it from the floor, had abandoned it.

We went on into the great room with its vaulted ceiling, where a half circle of chairs and settees surrounded an immense fireplace. High above us on the face of the stone chimney was a looming black shape. Although I could not discern its features in the gloom, I knew it to be the mounted head of an enormous bull elk. I perceived the dead scent of tanned furs and taxidermy which is associated with all such places, mixed with the odor of cigar smoke. At one end of the long rectangular dining table we saw the remains of Pontsylvania's final meal, flanked by his glass with three fingers of wine remaining in it and a single open bottle.

The high, arched opening into the broad corridor leading to the bedrooms appeared to me as a black and horrible yawning mouth. Kitty turned the dark lantern's slender shaft of light to pierce the darkness within.

We hesitated there. The silence was such that I could hear Kitty breathing. She said, very softly, "Should I go first, Hilda? I can make sure his face is covered and then it might not be so bad for you."

"Thank you Dear, but no," I said. "I will have to look at his face."

"Which room will he be in?"

"I don't know."

She took my hand and we went on together into the long corridor. As she lifted the lantern higher, I could vaguely discern the shapes of the various mounted game heads and racks of antlers which lined the high walls above our heads. I felt a quick thrill of fear on spying a line of light under one of the doors. Kitty's fingers tightened and she whispered, "Is someone here?"

"I think not," I said. "But this must be the room. Reynard said he lit a lamp." The door was not latched. I pushed it open slowly, filled with dread, and entered in to look upon the mortal remains of my unfortunate husband, Gerhard Richter von Plinth. The lamp burning on a stand at the bedside revealed his pallid, bloodless face. The staring eyes were like black pools and his mouth was open.

My fear left me then and I suddenly felt only tremendous pity. I knelt down beside the bed, sought his cold hand beneath the blanket and clasped it, exclaiming, "Oh, poor Gerhard! Poor, poor man."

Kitty drew closer and directed the beam of the dark lantern across the face, starkly illuminating the horrible eyes. "So," she said. "It is surely true, what Reynard said. He has been poisoned."

"Of course it is true," I replied. "I tried to warn him

against Manfred. He would never take me seriously. He thought I was just a silly hysterical woman. The poor, poor man. He could not conceive of a mind like that of my cousin. Even I did not realize the lengths to which he might go, though perhaps I should have. Raoul told me on the night of our wedding never to forget what he did to Fritzi." I broke down then and wept, both for my foolish husband and for Raoul's little dog.

Kitty allowed me a few minutes of this, then drew the blanket up to cover Pontsylvania's face. She laid her hand on my shoulder. "We should pray," she said. She knelt beside me. We bowed our heads and in unison spoke the *Pater Noster*, though I admit I faltered as I tried to utter the words "deliver us from evil." After we had spoken our *amens* and each made the sign of the cross, she rose and took me by the arm, gently drawing me away. "Hilda, Hilda! We must decide what we're going to do."

We went out into the great room and seated ourselves across from each other at the end of the table farthest away from Pontsylvania's leavings. We reached across the boards and clasped hands. The dark lantern stood on the flagstone floor and in the gloom I could not even discern the features of her face. I asked her, "What are you thinking of?"

"Firing the place, of course," she said. "Burn it down. I'm sorry about it, Hilda, but Reynard's life is of more matter than this old building. The remains of your husband will be found but it won't be known he was poisoned. It will appear as only a terrible accident."

I considered this plan with a sinking heart. "Kitty, I do so fear that a fire here in this remote place started at this time of night will not be noticed for hours. All these outbuildings will go up and we could have the whole forest ablaze. Consider also the Hoff family's cottage is not a quarter mile to the north along the road. We may precipitate a terrible disaster. There is also Sophie. It would be just too cruel to make her burn to death in the stable. We would have to let her loose, yet when found and identified, the fact of her escaping unscathed on the occasion of this supposedly accidental fire would have such a suspicious appearance. With Reynard, and only Reynard, known to have been here with Gerhard tonight, attention would turn directly to him.

"We can take Sophie away with your husband's saddle and bridle, and those we can hide until we can get rid of them later."

"Sophie herself is just as distinctive as her accoutrements."

"Then I can go right away and lead her up north of Weisspferde to the campground beyond the lake where the Travelers come and go. There's no doubt they would buy such a fine horse and if anyone ever came asking questions, you know they would give no answers."

"Kitty, if you do that you would not get to stop or sleep at all for two nights running at the least."

"Why, what do I care for stopping or sleeping as long as Reynard is safe?"

"But there is also this, Kitty: If it should happen you are seen anywhere along the way with Sophie by anyone who recognizes you, or even could just come forward and recall you later, it will appear as the very proof Reynard has set the fire and you are in conspiracy with him. There would be no other possible interpretation. I would not have you take such a risk."

"But then what else is there?"

"We could remove all evidence of what has taken place here."

"All?"

"Yes, absolutely all."

"Oh! But consider yourself, Hilda; your situation. Your husband cannot just disappear."

"I fear perhaps he must."

"But Hilda, what would be the way? I can't think we have time to bury everything; it would be such a task. We'd have to find tools and find a place, and then afterwards hide the place and put the tools back. We'd go home so filthy we'd have to make sure nobody sees our clothes and then we'd likely need to burn them. As for the river, you know how long is the ride from here to the boathouse."

"Yes, of course I do know, while close by stands the house of Hugo the lock-keeper who kindly keeps a watchful eye over our boats. No, it cannot be the river and we certainly do not have time to carry out a burial either."

"Hilda, we must set the fire!"

"Pray give me just one moment more to think." I held her hands tightly and bowed my head as I struggled with my conscience, for there was an image which had come fully formed into my mind before we had even seated ourselves at the table. It was no less dreadful than grave digging or sinking poor Pontsylvania's corpse in the river with an anchor chained to his belt, yet if one required to make a thing in the County of Eisenstein disappear so as never to be found again, I knew of nothing more likely to succeed and the distance we would be required to travel was not long. Could I steel myself to carry out such a terrible act and then live on with the consequences? Briefly my heart shrank in horror from these questions, but then my mind was overtaken with a rapidly shifting series of memories: Reynard leading my pony when my little legs were too short to reach the stirrups. Reynard and Raoul together returning triumphant from a day's fishing, not with trout but their creels entirely stuffed with morels. Reynard, Raoul, Kitty and myself up on Wachterburg on an autumn evening, telling stories of fairies and ancient times by candlelight; then following after this, a great full moon rising above the trees as we walked home in quiet bliss, Kitty and Reynard on either side of me and holding my hands, for I was the little one. Kitty in green, her hair covered with a chaplet of white crocheted lace, singing *Ave Maria* in the church on Christmas Eve. Reynard gathering up five kittens from the stables and slipping them into my bedroom in the early morning as I still slept, that I might wake to find them frolicking about the room. My dear father and Everard Manx sitting up late before the fire in the back parlor, smoking old-fashioned long clay pipes and talking of rabbits, crops and cows.

I was truly sorry for Pontsylvania, sorry above all for his mother, even sorry for Max, but Gerhard von Plinth was now beyond all aid. Should Reynard Manx also succumb to the evil of my family's curse, the machinations of my wretched cousin, how then would I live with myself? Truly there should be nothing I would not do.

I released Kitty's hands and rose from the table. "There is a way. We must be quick. Go in the pantry and find a sack. Put all the food in it and the dirty dishes. What remains of the wine, pour it out on the ground and mind you do not let it touch you, then put the bottle and the glass as well into the sack. Clear everything up as fast as you can but let nothing be missed. Do also look into the room where Reynard was sleeping. See he has left nothing behind and Manfred has not put anything there. Be looking out for any small medicine bottle or flask. If that is here it may be hidden yet not any too well hidden I should think. I will return to my husband's room, find his portmanteau and make sure all his effects are gathered into it, including his boots which I do hope can be forced to fit. Then I'm going out to the butchering shed to look for the thing we need."

"And what is the thing we need?"

"A chain. A good strong iron chain, with a hook."

XII. The aftermath of terrible deeds

A faint glow heralding the imminent dawn could be perceived along the edge of the eastern horizon when Kitty and I hurried, stumbling and exhausted, up the hill path from the stables to the Eisenstein manor house. In the back hallway, we kicked off our boots and then we embraced. I kissed her warm cheeks. "I love you so very much, Kitty Dear," I said. "Get to your bed and try to rest."

"You'll not need help with Max?"

"No, not now. I must change clothes and nurse him straightaway. Or nurse him first and then change, if I find him crying."

"You will explain to Reynard?

"Certainly."

"And when they come?"

"I will be ready."

Boots in hand, I hastened up the stairs. I went quickly down the long gallery on the second floor where a series of three low lamps burned through the night, then entered the dark stairwell of my tower. I felt my way upwards with a hand on the wall. On the landing I could see the faint escape of light around the door. Silently raising the latch, I opened it slightly and then was halted, startled by what I heard from within. A fine tenor voice was softly singing.

"Baby sweet,
your mother is the duchess.
Naughty little baby,
your mother is a queen.
Baby sweet,
you mother is an angel.
Naughty little baby,
go to sleep and dream, dream, dream.
Go to sleep and dream
of the duchess, the angel, the queen.

Baby sweet,
the moon it shines upon her.
Naughty little baby,
the sun shines on her too.
Baby sweet,
the stars shine all around her.
Naughty little baby,
go to sleep and dream, dream, dream.
Go to sleep and dream
of the duchess, the angel, the queen."

I rattled the latch a bit to signal my arrival and spare Reynard any awkwardness, then entered and shut the door behind me. He was seated in the rocker by the fireplace, tilted back, holding my baby boy upon his chest. Max's curly head lay on his shoulder. He was rubbing the child's back while with one foot against the fender he kept the chair gently in motion.

Without yet speaking, for I was determined to forget nothing in my fatigue, I went directly to my writing desk and found pencil and paper with which to set down a short note. I folded this twice in half and slipped it into a side pocket of Reynard's deerskin vest. "When you go down," I said, "you must please put that in the kitchen straightaway before you go to bed. It is for Madam Baeder. I've written to say the Duke is not at the lodge and she need not go."

He replied in a low voice for sake of the drowsing boy on his chest. "I shall deliver it as you say, Madam, though I can scarce imagine going to bed."

I fell into the slipper chair at the other end of the hearth. Not since the night of Max's birth had I ever felt such a profound exhaustion.

Reynard rose and gently delivered Max into my arms. Max, on feeling my presence, began to whimper. There had been a shawl of crocheted linen hanging over the back of the rocker. Reynard considerately passed this to me, then crossed to the far side of the room and stood before a dark window as if gazing out.

"How has he been?" I asked.

"Mostly just sleeping but this last hour he's gotten a bit restless. No doubt he'll be happy to have you and Kitty back. I've changed his nappy and I'm sure you'll laugh when you inspect my work. I have no experience."

He was silent for a minute or two while I attended to Max. Finally he asked, "Is the bailiff on the way, then?

"No," I said.

"But you have been to the magistrate?"

"No."

"You have sent someone, then."

"No."

"You will be sending someone."

"I will not."

His decorum abandoning him, he turned his head to look at me. Max lay sighing softly beneath the shawl. "What is to happen, then?"

"Nothing, except that my husband's guests will be arriving and I must explain he has been urgently called away."

"Called away?"

"Yes."

"What . . . have you done?"

"I have followed Manfred's example. If he and all signs of his presence could completely disappear from the lodge, so then could everything else."

Reynard now swung about to face me directly, staring wide-eyed with astonishment. "And where did everything else go?"

I lifted a hand to cover my eyes for a moment. I had been steadfast through it all, yet suddenly now a reaction set in and I began to shiver. "Up Wachterberg to the castle and down the well. It is utterly vile and horrible yet it was the safest way I could think of. While I am remembering it, I must mention to you one of the hoisting chains will have gone missing from the butchering shed at the lodge. We put it to use, with the strength of the horses, for the heavy work. The final task for which we employed it was to pull the well cover back into place, so we were left with it. There wasn't time to return it to the lodge but I did think best to be rid of it so I threaded it down the privy hole in the *danzker*. I'm not certain it made it all the way through and into the river, but I am quite sure it all went in and disappeared.

There was profound silence as he continued to stare at me. I felt I must have shocked him deeply. I went on, "It was entirely my idea and my decision, not Kitty's, and a terrible, terrible thing to do. I pray you will not think too harshly of me, Reynard."

"Most certainly not. I do assure you, Madam, you have my highest regard."

I drew out two items from the pocket of my skirt. One was a heavy ring of gold and black onyx, the other a folded half sheet of stationery. With my tremulous hand, I offered him the paper. "You must see this. I found it in one of my husband's saddle bags."

He opened it and held it by the lamp on the mantelpiece. "A note from Mr. Klench stating he will join His Grace the Duke at the Eisenstein hunting lodge in the morning on the 22nd. Meaning this morning now just beginning."

"My poor husband of course was never in receipt of that. Manfred put it into the saddle bag while he was already dying, or dead. Now that you've seen it, burn it, please."

He held it in the top of the lamp chimney until it caught fire, then set it down in the grate and watched as it was consumed. He asked, "Did you chance to come upon anything along the lines of some little black bottle marked with skull and crossbones? With His Grace's remains taken away I have scant fear of it for myself, yet on general principle I would not have any poison left lying about in the lodge. I turned out all the pockets of my peppermint-stinking coat but there was nothing."

"Kitty did find an apothecary's vial in the pantry with a small remainder of some dark tincture. On a low shelf behind a tea tin, so placed in hiding while at the same time quite easily come upon. There were only traces of a label which had been torn off. I think almost certainly that must have been it. It has gone with the rest we removed. We left the lodge appearing as though not visited by anyone at any recent time."

He turned his gaze to the ring which still lay in the palm of my hand. "I recall His Grace was wearing that."

"It is the signet of Pontsylvania. It belongs to Max. I will put it away. It's safe enough. I can say my husband left it behind here last night."

"Here?"

"Oh, yes. He changed his mind, you see, about spending the night at the hunting lodge. He found himself so anxious to see me, he never went there at all but came at night directly to this house, to me, his wife. His horse, tack and hunting gear I have brought here where he obviously has left them behind. All the other effects he carried he has

. . . taken with him."

"You positively amaze me. I don't know why your mad cousin tries to match wits with you." A painful sadness then fell as a dark shadow over his countenance. "I must say though, I am so deeply sorry about all of this. In truth I cannot begin to fathom how terrible it must be for you. You will be in my prayers."

"Thank you, Reynard."

He turned again to the window. "The sun is rising. I must go down."

"Reynard, when Manfred arrives and for the time he is in residence, I require you to be out and busy elsewhere. Eisenstein will extend every courtesy to him and the other hunting gentlemen and all their needs will be attended to, but you will have no part in it. I don't know for how long they will inflict themselves upon us, but as soon as they've gone, I must return immediately to Strelsau."

He looked down at the floor. "Yes. Of course you must. I am tremendously obliged to you for what you've done."

"You owe me nothing, Reynard, and on behalf of my wretched family, I sincerely apologize to you. In addition, should you wish to leave us, I will exert any influence I possess to gain you a generous severance and I am confident my brother will join me in this."

"Hilda! Is that your wish, that I should go?"

"No, it is not my wish, but I thought it might be yours."

"I'm sure I would prefer to remain. God bless you, Your Grace." He went out.

Some ten minutes may have passed while I lay limp in the chair with Max sighing in my arms. Then I heard a faint rattle of the latch and the door opened just enough to admit Muffin. I glimpsed Reynard's hands depositing her gently upon the floor. The door closed behind her. She trundled her fat, fluffy body across the rug and came to rub her face against my skirt.

XIII. I begin my career as an actress

At 10:30 in the morning, four mounted gentlemen appeared in the drive. Having seen them from the window, I hastened out and waited at the bottom of the steps. Kitty followed with Max in her arms and seated herself on one of the stone benches in the portico, a vantage point from which she could discreetly listen and observe. I turned back to look up at her once; she softly spoke but one word. "Courage."

The four advanced together with Manfred in the lead. Drawing up beside me, he opened the proceedings with a hearty greeting. "My dearest Cousin Hilda, good morning to you!"

Mustering up the most cordial of tones, I replied, "Good morning, Manfred. And it's a pleasure to see you again, Mr. Trundelheimer." I thus addressed one gentleman I had previously been introduced to by my husband. As such pleasantries were carried forward to their natural conclusion, I was introduced to the other two gentlemen and forgot their names instantly.

Manfred's face was drawn and his eyes rimmed with pink, betraying his lack of sleep. Imagining my own burning eyes must look the same, I shielded them from the sun with my hand as I looked up at him. And so the opening volley was discharged: "Well, Hilda," he said, "What have you done with Pontsylvania?"

His choice of words struck me as a sharp blow, yet I showed him only a tentative smile to denote my polite puzzlement at this peculiar question. "Done with him?"

"He was to meet us at the hunting lodge but he is not there. He had expressed to me his distinct intention to sleep there last night and be prepared to receive us this morning. Where is he?"

"I am so sorry," I said, "I had meant to send a boy over to the lodge with a message. I should have done it earlier but I was awake much of the night and I've overslept. I am also very sorry to have to tell you Gerhard is not here after all, Manfred. He has had to go to Vienna."

This was no doubt a shocking counter-strike, and he blinked. "Vienna? But I've just looked in at the stables here, Hilda. Sophie is there, and his saddle."

"Well, yes. He came in riding Sophie but he certainly wasn't going to ride her all the way to Vienna and back. He left here riding a hack."

"Was he going to get a train?"

"I suppose so. It seems most likely.

"From where?"

"I don't know. We had only a few hours together and there were far more important things to discuss than trains."

"Did he take his guns?"

"His pistols, surely. His rifle I believe he will have left here. Did you wish to borrow it?"

His face had gone deathly pale save for the sharp pink of his eyelids. His lips drew down into a pout while his hands at the reigns twisted nervously. "Can you expect me to accept this preposterous story, that he has made plans to meet us here at Eisenstein but then gone off to Vienna?"

"Why, yes, because it is TRUE, Manfred. He arrived here quite late and said he had received a telegram. Some urgent business matter requiring his presence. If I were to hazard a guess I would say there might have been some highly significant contract to be negotiated and signed as soon as possible, though I do only speculate."

"A telegram. Where would he have got a telegram?"

"Wherever he stopped last night I would imagine but I really don't know. I supposed he must have sent some query from wherever he was and got a reply to it. I didn't ask for an explanation. It was of no interest to me."

"But a telegram from whom?"

"I have no idea. He didn't show it to me and again, I did not ask. We had very little time, Manfred, and there was certainly no room within our discourse for details about his boring business dealings or trains or telegrams. He stayed with me a few hours and then rode out this morning at 8:oo o'clock."

"Stayed with you." Manfred's tone bore the faintest tinge of sarcasm.

"Yes, and I was so tired after he left, I remained late in

bed. Again, I do apologize, Manfred. Now if you'd care to return to the lodge with your friends, I'll have people attend to you. Mr. Ricard will be at your disposal for the hunting and the Braun boy will be sent over with some nice provisions as quickly as can be done. No doubt you are all hungry after your long ride. I do hope you will enjoy yourselves."

"When is Pontsylvania coming back?"

"He didn't know exactly. He had a hope of returning in time to get some hunting in with you and the other gentlemen but he was not at all sure. He thought it might even be as long as two weeks, at the worst. He asked me to tell you, you should go right ahead with your sport and on no account wait for him."

"Where in Vienna?"

"I do not KNOW, Manfred. The only other information I can provide to you is that he was extremely annoyed about the spoiling of his plans. You can be assured he would VERY much prefer to be in the woods shooting animals in the company of his friends than be wherever he is now."

He stared pointedly at me for a protracted moment, his lips compressed in an expression of dogged frustration. I waited patiently for his next question. Then suddenly, as if at the quick turning over of a new card, he was smiling again. "Ah well, it is too bad, but it can't be helped. We shall have to carry on without him. Thank you, Hilda my Dear, for your kind assistance in providing hospitality to our friends."

Further pleasantries ensued, with welcomings and thanks all around, until at last they turned the horses and rode away.

Kitty came down to me and gave me Max, as she knew it would comfort me to hold him. "Neatly done, Hilda," she said. "He doesn't know what has happened. I don't think he's even quite sure the Duke really died last night."

"Oh, I think he is sure. And he'll only need a few minutes to think things through before he understands just how his plot has been foiled. The only thing he doesn't know is where my poor husband's remains now lie."

"Let us not speak of it again," said Kitty. "Not ever."

"Yes, save that I must speak of it to Raoul," I replied. "Just once. I need not mention you."

She broke into a smile for a moment. "Oh, are you going to tell him you did it all by yourself? You must give me the credit I'm due. And I do trust in your brother. We are all in it together, Hilda. We have always been."

"Well I do hope Manfred will be thoroughly miserable over these next few days. He loathes hunting, you know, though he pretends otherwise for the benefit of his manly friends."

"Does he really?"

"Oh, I am sure of it. It's much too uncomfortable and messy."

XIV. Return to Strelsau ✤ Help arrives, with shocking news

We traveled from Zenda to Strelsau on the train. I found a newspaper left in our compartment and read the announcement of the impending date of the King's formal betrothal ceremony, lauded as glorious news for the future of Ruritania and the Elphberg line. I felt sorry for Flavia. I also felt sorry for Henriette as she valiantly suppressed the signs of her grief at our removal from Eisenstein.

Arriving at Pontsylvania House, I was inexpressibly relieved to find that Pontsylvania's mother had left two days prior for a respite in Menton. How I had dreaded facing her with my story about his mysterious business trip. By the time she returned, it would be entirely evident he was missing and possibly I might also have Raoul. I desperately wanted Raoul. I sent Kitty to the telegraph office.

I had meant to feign illness in order to retire from society. However pretending proved unnecessary as I fell into the throes of a nervous reaction. I suffered from insomnia and when I did manage to sleep, there were repetitive dreams in which a smirking Manfred would speak affectionate words to me in an endless variety of settings as he offered me glasses of wine or open boxes of bonbons which I dared not taste, while I would be miserably speechless when pressed to explain why. Strangely enough, however, I did not dream of Wachterberg or of the well. Somehow my deeds performed there in the deep of the night under the cryptic beam of the dark lantern had eclipsed and dispelled my childhood imaginings. I, myself, had become more terrible than the ghosts of *Schloss Eisenstein.*

I could hardly drag myself up again in the mornings. My indomitably spirited Kitty endeavored to provide me all possible comfort. She conceived the idea of rearranging all the furnishings of my apartments, that the sights before my eyes might be less remindful of the past. This was a help yet the appearance of the bedstead in particular, though it stood in a different place, still appalled me. I slept in my dressing room. The tapestry there which I had previously so enjoyed was taken down and put away, although I did look down upon it as it lay upon the floor waiting to be rolled up, recalling how much I had loved it, vowing in my heart I would have it again one day.

My adorable Max, of course, was the anchor that held me against being swept away into darkness, for he cared about none of it. He cared only about me, and Kitty, and the wonder of his very own little toes.

Manfred paid a call after a fortnight, to be informed I

was ill and Pontsylvania not yet returned. He left his card. In five more days, he called again, heard the same report again and left another card, this time with the small notation *"always wishing the best"* added in graceful script.

Another week, and I received a note delivered by messenger from his club:

Dearest H,

I am so sorry to know you have not been well. I am at your disposal if I may be of service in any way.

With my fondest regards,

M

I set fire to this vile epistle on the cold and empty grate of my bedroom fireplace. One more week and a box of white lilies was delivered with his initials on the card and the notation *"with enduring regard."* A horrible realization was coming to me. I had at first hoped, even assumed, the impossibly tangled circumstances in which we now found ourselves would dissuade Manfred from any further pursuit of my affections. But it had not. He was actually hoping we might become united in a shared complicity around the elimination of my husband. Such was my fear of possibly encountering him, I did not dare leave the house.

My father came to dinner. I had hoped to be comforted by his presence but the weight of my terrible secret lay between us, such that I felt we were separated by a distorting wall of glass. He expressed concern at my appearance. I told him Max was teething and I was therefore fatigued. I did not think he believed me, if for no other reason than his tactful avoidance of any mention of my husband's absence, a circumstance I myself made no effort to explain. He urged me to visit him soon. With fresh pangs of guilt I falsely promised to do so. I could only imagine Manfred coming to the door of the Eisen town house while I was there and having himself ushered into my presence. I had to assume he had at least one spy among the staff at Pontsylvania House. Kitty personally posted all my letters.

❧ ❧ ❧ ❧

When I could put it off no longer, I sat down with an anguished heart and wrote to the Dowager Duchess Agathe, informing her of her son's trip to Vienna and his failure to return or inform me of his plans. Most horribly, I entreated her to pass on to me any information about his arrangements he might have provided to her but not to me. I wrote next to Strelsau's Commissioner of Police with a request for a confidential meeting. I sat poised in my misery, pen in hand, to write to my father and ask him to accompany me to that dreaded appointment, when Kitty came in. She was smiling broadly. "Good news for a change," she said.

Dropping my pen on the blotter, I held my throbbing head in my hands. "What good news could there possibly be?"

"Mr. Eisen is here."

"My father?" I said stupidly.

"Your brother. Don't forget to lock up your desk."

I found Raoul in the lesser drawing room, swinging an

114

ecstatic, giggling Max up in the air and shouting, "Wheeee! Wheeee!" On being handed back to Kitty, Max was enraged, went red in the face and began to cry. We all laughed and then I threw my arms about Raoul's neck. "Hilda, Hilda, Hilda!" Following a protracted embrace, he held me out at arm's length.

"You've turned so brown," I said. "It makes you all the more debonair. You are well?"

"Perfectly well," he replied, "but I see you are not. You look as if you'd been chained in a dungeon for months. And why the summons, Hilda Dear? Can it possibly have anything to do with these gruesome goings-on at Zenda?"

"What do you mean by that?"

"Good heavens, Hilda, you're positively blanching. What have I said? Here, do sit down."

"No, no; I need not sit, but what 'gruesome goings-on' at Zenda?"

"How are you not aware? It's all over the streets. I first heard about it in the train from Trieste. Black Michael is dead."

"What?"

He spoke it out gently and slowly, as if to a child, "The Grand Duke of Strelsau, generally known as Black Michael, younger half-brother to our esteemed King, is no longer living."

"Why, what has happened to him?"

"It is reported he was killed in his chateau at Zenda by that bounder Hentzau. A fair fight between gentlemen one may hope, but it was certainly not a formal duel. Quite impromptu."

"Rupert von Hentzau? Do you know him?"

"Everyone knows him."

"But was he not one of the Grand Duke's closest friends?"

"Certainly. Therefore they were acquainted with all the same women. I would lay a handsome wager there was a woman behind it. But then, I would wager even more we will never hear the truth of it. Secrets of State, you know.

"To have killed the King's brother! What will happen to him?"

"Nothing, unless they first catch him and drag him back. He has disappeared like a puff of smoke. Surely at this moment he is no longer within the borders of Ruritania. So, Hilda Dear, did you need me to come all the way from Cairo that you might be informed about events at Zenda?" He winked at me.

In the last moments at my desk, I had written these words on a small scrap of paper: *"We must speak at length where we cannot be overheard."* Saying nothing, I placed it in his hand.

He perused it, looked up at me with raised eyebrows, then stepped to the fireplace where a small coal fire was burning. He dropped the bit of paper. We watched it burst into flame and quickly vanish, and then he offered me his arm. "I've been much too long sitting in trains," he said. "Come, Hilda, let us have a good long stroll in the gardens while you bring my up to date on all your news."

XV. Raoul's career as an actor

From this time forward, Raoul was at my side in all things. I had at first felt guilty for drawing him into my unsavory intrigue, but he was quite unfazed. He lied with urbane confidence to the Commissioner of Police, to my husband's attorney, to my husband's bank manager, to the Dowager Duchess Agathe, and to our father. A power of attorney was granted to him for the management of financial and legal affairs on behalf of Max and myself. Private investigators were retained in both Ruritania and Austria to trace Pontsylvania's movements after he had ridden away from Eisenstein. A generous monetary reward was offered for information resulting in the location of his person, effects or remains. This of course resulted in various reports of false sightings and discoveries of misconstrued personal items and papers of no actual significance with regard to Pontsylvania or his disappearance. Some of these efforts were so absurd, Raoul found them a source of hilarity. Raoul's had always been a cheerful nature yet he was also possessed of a rather dark sense of humor.

Manfred caused a bottle of a rare and costly wine to be delivered to me with the note, *"Looking forward to your company in happier days ahead."* I gazed upon it in horror and disgust, uncertain if he'd sent it for purposes of courting me or killing me. I promptly emptied it into a drain.

The day following this noxious communication, Raoul appeared in high spirits at breakfast. Slathering butter over a slice of toast, he said, "I spent three long and dreary hours at Manfred's club last night."

I poured tea for him. "You are not a member of Manfred's club."

"No, but I have acquaintances who are. I contrived to have myself invited in as a guest. The evening was for the most part an abominable bore, but I did achieve my objective."

"Which was?"

"Why, to catch a moment alone with our dear cousin so that I might straighten his cravat for him whilst making mention of bodily harm. I had not threatened Manfred with bodily harm for a number of years and I realized I had been sadly remiss. The man is such a craven physical coward. Hence he doth resort to poisoning his rivals as the wives of the Ottoman Sultans have been known to do."

I was unable to return his ironic smile. Instead my eyes were stung with tears. He laid his hand gently upon mine. "Come, Hilda. Do not lose heart. It's an absolutely horrible world. It is also a wonderful world and you are very young yet. Some day this will all be as a bad dream of things that happened long ago. Or on the other hand, some day we may, by comparison, think of this as one of our jollier periods."

I did smile then. "Oh, surely not!"

"There's my brave girl. Now, this preparation in the brown crock is an excellent new marmalade from Scotland. You must try it."

XVI. The royal wedding

The etiquette books do not inform us on the proper attire at a royal wedding for ladies whose husbands have mysteriously disappeared. I decided on something like half mourning and had a gown and jacket made up in dove gray with a black *soutache* edge and a high neckline. I needed only the one dress as I would attend the ceremony but not the ball.

I took my place in our Eisen family box in the cathedral with my father at my left and Raoul at my right. Manfred and Aunt Olympia arrived some minutes later. She was first seated at our father's other side, leaving Manfred to either stay with his mother and take the space remaining by the gate or step over the feet of all the rest of us, this second option being obviously indefensible. Raoul held my hand in a firm and comforting grasp as we waited in the silence of deep reverence, heads bowed and eyes cast down in accordance with the solemnity of the occasion.

I did risk looking up for a moment when King

Rudolph and his attendants entered the chancel and took their places. I was shocked to see how very much changed he was, appearing frail and ill, with hollowed eyes and cheeks, his dress uniform fitting loosely on his shrunken frame. The weight of the many rows of medals upon his chest seemed to me as nearly too much for him to bear, for his shoulders were stooped. The death of his brother had evidently affected him terribly.

We all rose to bear witness as Princess Flavia processed to the altar on the arm of her father, Axel von Turmen, styled King Ragnar IV of Gothe-Saxeberg. He was a tall, erect and distinguished man of military bearing, his wiry reddish hair cut *en brosse* and shot through with strands of silver. Flavia was magnificent in her pure white raiment, the extravagant train streaming like a waterfall over the wide, blue-carpeted steps as she ascended the dais. Near the close of an arduously long ceremony, the folding back of her long veil revealed a diamond-brooched sash crossing her breast in the green, white and blue of Gothe-Saxeberg. With her pale and noble face, crowned by a pile of glorious copper tresses banded within a tall gold tiara set with emeralds and pearls, she appeared to me as like the classical image of Pallas Athena. She was hardly of this world in her glory.

During the recessional she passed so close to us, I could see her eyes. They were the eyes of a woman walking to the scaffold.

XVII. Pontsylvania's secret

I sat in Pontsylvania's study with Raoul, who was seated at the desk. The entire vast surface was covered with piles of paper, with the exception of one small corner on which his cigarette smoldered in the hideous elephant foot ashtray.

"I believe I have rifled and rummaged through every single thing," he said, "provided there are no secret panels or hollowed-out books we've yet to discover. For the most part it's all quite ordinary and above board and all is in excellent trim. Pontsylvania wasn't one for running up debt nor has he been gambling away Max's inheritance in secret or any such thing. He seems to have been a prudent and methodical sort of fellow. I give him credit. To have the managing of a ridiculously large fortune is not an easy situation for every man to maintain."

"Why did you say, 'for the most part'?"

He hesitated. "Hilda, I must ask you a terribly impertinent question. Did you love Gerhard von Plinth? I mean, were you IN love with the man?"

I looked down at my folded hands in my lap. "No. I was not in love, nor did I love. I had genuinely hoped I would love him, but no. He seemed very gallant before we married but I realize now that was a sort of mating dance and not reflective of his true character. He was not especially intelligent nor was he sensible of my feelings. He was also highly susceptible to flattery, a weakness Manfred exploited with ease and which I found painful to witness. I suppose the worst of it was that I had expected him to be my protector yet he proved no such thing. He paid my personal secretary to act as his spy as if this were an ordinary and necessary thing for any powerful man to do with a wife who had never told him a single lie or committed dissemblances of any kind. Yet at the same time and despite all my warnings and entreaties, he allowed Manfred to invade this house to the extent it was almost as if he were in residence. He did give me Maxie though, and being a pompous fool is not a crime deserving of the death penalty, and so I am truly terribly sorry for what happened to him. Now I suspect I have given you the answer you were hoping for, so you may tell me why you asked your impertinent question."

"He was making a regular monthly withdrawal from the bank, quite a substantial amount. It was certainly nothing he couldn't afford but the reason for it wasn't readily apparent. I have investigated the matter of to what those funds were being applied."

"And?"

"He was keeping a separate establishment. Very discreet. A Parisian woman."

"For how long?"

"Since before you were first introduced to him, Hilda. Not very long before, apparently. Two or three months."

"Good heavens! Did they . . . do they . . ."

"Have children? Mercifully not. However she had been a hat check girl at the opera when they met and of course on entering into her relation with him she gave up her position as well as any other arrangements she may have had. She was entirely dependent on him and has fallen into terrible straights. According to my sources, she now sleeps on a cot in apartments from which every stick of furniture has been sold and is days away from being put out on the street. It is said she's a remarkably pretty woman now twenty-six years of age and there are other gentlemen who would have been pleased to step in, but she has adamantly refused to shift her allegiance."

"But why, when she has obviously been abandoned?"

"Because she has been holding out hope that he will come back."

"Oh, but this is dreadful!"

"Yes, it is, rather."

"Raoul, you are a man. Did you know of this? Before, I mean."

"As God is my witness, I did not know. I suppose if I had not been out of the country so much in recent years, I'd have been more likely to discover it. I greatly regret my failure to find it out and for that I do sincerely apologize to you, Hilda."

"And our father . . ."

"Has absolutely no idea and we shall never speak of it."

"I do wonder what Pontsylvania can have said to her about our marriage."

"Oh, one can easily speculate what sort of things he might have said. That he was honor bound by an awesome duty far greater than himself, steeped in the blood of centuries of generations von Plinth both past and future, to sacrifice and mortify himself upon the alter of a suitable marriage within the peerage for the sake of the Duchy. That you're an awful woman and his mother chose you . . ."

"Good heavens, DID she choose me? Agathe, I mean."

Raoul smiled gently, shaking his head. "No, no, no, Hilda. She approved of you certainly, but it was Pontsylvania who charted his own course and Pontsylvania who chose you, of that I am quite sure. If you but reflect upon it for a moment you must realize he was not a man to ever see himself advised by any woman. When the Dowager Duchess proposed the introduction to our father, she was merely acting as his agent."

"This poor girl; have you seen her?"

"I have not. My inclination is to do something for her but I will only act if you agree."

"What do you suggest?"

"That I explain to her directly we have undertaken exhaustive measures to trace Pontsylvania without a crumb of success and that we believe him to be dead due to some unknown crime or misadventure occurring as he traveled alone on a business trip to Austria. And then I would propose to pay her creditors and her train fare, with some other expenses at a generous amount, if she will agree to leave Ruritania. Perhaps she would wish to return to France.”

“I agree. When can you go?”

“Immediately, if you like.”

“Please. I would not want her suffering to go on for one more minute.”

“I am so sorry if this is a hurtful revelation for you, Hilda.”

“I’m not at all sure that it is. I did worry about being such a failure, you know. As a wife. I see now my concerns in that regard were all quite irrelevant. Raoul, please tell her I bear her no ill will.”

“I will tell her. Hilda, there is another thing. If I do not return to Cairo almost immediately I will lose my posting.”

“Do you need it?”

“Not exactly.”

“You want to go back.”

“I do want to go. Very much.”

I felt myself instantly dissolving. Hot tears coursed down my cheeks.”

“Hilda, Hilda!” He leapt from his chair and rounded the desk. Going down on one knee, he clasped my hands between his. “Hilda, I have been thinking about this. You cannot go back to Eisenstein yet.”

“No, no, not yet!”

“But you cannot stay a prisoner in this Strelsau hellhole of sybaritic luxury with Manfred breathing heavily through the mail slot.”

I could not help laughing while at the same time, I continued to weep.

"Hilda," he went on, "Maxie doesn't need to put on pants and start learning his letters for ages yet. You will find much can change with time, perhaps even in a single year. I do want to go back to Cairo and I think you should come with me. You and Maxie and Kitty and Henriette."

XVIII. An awkward parting

The ensuing period was a flurry of planning and packing. I was at my desk perusing one of my numerous lists when Kitty entered with a note in her hand. "My brother is in Strelsau. At the house of the Count, your father. Only until tomorrow. He has brought something for a signature."

"You will want to see him."

"Oh yes, very much."

"Of course you shall go. Does he know of our plans as yet?"

"I would think not. I have written, but my letter I assume is not yet arrived at Eisenstein, while he will have passed it coming in the opposite direction. Is there anything you want me to say to him?"

"Let me think a moment." I kept her waiting for some time but I was not really thinking so much as struggling in a whirling storm of conflicted emotions. At last I said, "I will speak to him myself. Right away. It will not take long. As soon as I come back, we shall send you over and you must stay as long as you wish. Would you please ask Helmut to step out and find a cab?" This was to be the only time, other than my attendance at Flavia's wedding, that I would set foot outside Pontsylvania House before we left to board the train for Trieste.

On arriving at the Eisen town house, I asked that Reynard be summoned to the breakfast room. As it was late in the afternoon, I thought this a setting where we might meet in propriety yet without interruption. I seated myself facing the door across the long, polished table. Gleaming silver chafing dishes in a row upon the mahogany sideboard appeared to me as expectantly waiting. The silence was touched only by the soft ticking of a painted clock on which a winged Eros hovered eternally over his beloved Psyche. The minutes passed slowly.

Reynard entered. "You wished to see me, Your Grace."

"Yes, Reynard, thank you. Please close the door and please sit."

He took the chair directly across the table from me. I sensed he was ill at ease, yet he carried always a certain unassailable dignity.

"As we are old friends and have suffered through much together," I said, "I ask that you call me by my name."

He did not answer but sat quite still, his head slightly tilted in inquiry, returning my gaze with his clear blue eyes, waiting.

"Reynard, it seems that I cannot be anywhere. It is unthinkable at this time to return to Eisenstein yet my life here in Strelsau is also absolutely intolerable."

"I do understand, Hilda. I am so very sorry."

"My brother is returning to his post in Cairo and I have determined to accompany him. Kitty will come with me. Henriette is leaving my employ, as she does not wish to go."

"For how long?"

"I don't know. Obviously I must eventually return so Max can be educated and take his place in society. But it may be quite a long time. I hope you can forgive me for taking Kitty so far away. It is her decision and I am deeply grateful. I don't know what I should do without her. In time I will bring her back to you, I do promise."

He continued to sit perfectly still, his gaze direct and unwavering. I went on, "Reynard, you have endured so much. Is it not time you sought some happiness for yourself? Should you not marry? Perhaps Henriette . . ." I was appalled to see his eyes suddenly flood with tears. "Oh, please forgive me if I have said too much."

The brimming tears did not fall as he seemed to hold them back by the very force of his will. I quickly drew a folded handkerchief from my waistband and placed it on the table before him. He did not look down but his fingers closed over it. He spoke softly, almost in a whisper, but with an intense vehemence. "I shall not marry Henriette. I shall not marry. How should I marry while you go on like this, married to a dead man yet not a widow, and all for my sake?"

"But it is not your fault!"

"What difference should it make to me, Hilda, that it is not my fault?"

The door opened and my father stepped in. "Ah, good morning, Hilda. There you are, Manx."

XIX.   Respite in a foreign land

The time of our sojourn in Egypt is a dream of very long ago, yet there remains a jumble of striking scenes still vivid in my memory. I saw wondrous things, abundant beauties beyond all imagination, some created by the hands of men and some by the hands of the Divine. Beside these myriad *tableaux* of enchantment, I witnessed want and even squalor such as I had never known in Ruritania. Egypt opened my eyes to the world.

We were met at the docks by Raoul's great friend James Woodbury, who was an *attaché* to the British Legation. James was to become a constant in our lives. He was a companionable and entertaining young man: well educated, courtly in his manners, urbane and sharply witty. He was fluent not only in his native English but in French and Arabic as well. His German was partial and I came to understand this had come to him by way of his association with Raoul. I also observed Raoul to be entirely fluent in both French and Arabic. The French was not a surprise but the Arabic I had never imagined.

Within a few months I was thinking in French myself, for I found this was the first language in which any shopkeeper or new acquaintance, whether European or Egyptian, would address me. I was at first perplexed by this, as Egypt was a Protectorate of Great Britain nominally under the rule of the Ottoman Turks. Raoul explained that for many decades the French had pursued extensive business interests in Egypt. The Turkish-Egyptian monarchy was heavily in debt to both British and French creditors and the French government even participated with Britain in management of the nation's finances. Of most particular significance was the construction and continued operation of the Suez Canal by a French company. Thus were France and Egypt so intertwined, the wealthy elite among the native families of Egypt were long in the habit of sending their sons to be educated in Paris and traversing the Mediterranean by steamship to enjoy the amenities of Monte Carlo and the *Côte d'Azur*.

In Cairo, Raoul leased for us a charming old villa consisting of a pair of lofty two-story structures facing each other across a large garden. High walls entirely obscured from the streets our peaceful secret world, which could only be entered through one of two solidly built gates. The arched front gate was tall, brightly painted and ornately studded with huge iron nails, the back gate a sort of postern, a low door through which two people might pass abreast and always kept barred from within. Kitty, Max and I occupied a suite of airy and spacious upstairs rooms while Raoul was established in ground floor apartments on the opposite side of the garden. From my own commodious private balcony I looked down upon an orange tree, a lemon tree and a colorful, fragrant display of flowering shrubbery. The center of the garden was paved with stone and in the midst of this a fountain, tiled in brilliant shades of blue, produced the constant, soothing sound of trickling water. Encounters with small lizards in the house were disconcerting at first but we did become accustomed to them and in time began to playfully assign names to them. We did quickly learn vigilance with regard to scorpions and even snakes, though there were surely at least twenty lizard visitations for any one of these.

There were several French *couturiers* in Cairo. Kitty and I had new wardrobes made, consisting of cotton dresses with light gloves and straw hats. Having dispensed with the services previously provided by Henriette, we hired a laundress for two days a week and otherwise took care of our own things and dressed each other's hair. When we dined on the terrace at Shepheard's we were sometimes taken to be sisters. It was all rather a lark and quite refreshing.

James accompanied us on most of our excursions. We made for a most congenial sort of family group: Kitty, Max, Raoul, James and I. During the second year of our stay, there was a time of crisis when Max contracted a fever so terrible we feared for his life. It was James who brought to us, in the middle of the night, a competent French physician who provided the necessary medicine. I came to dearly love James. He was neither married nor engaged yet not without several hopeful admirers within the European community of Cairo. I did at one time suggest to Kitty she might do well to set her cap for him but she only laughed, stating that although she did hold him in high esteem he was not of her type. I did not press the matter as there is no accounting for these things.

In January, when the heat drove out of Cairo everyone who could possibly get away, we would rent one of the private house boats, a *dahabeyah*, and take a leisurely cruise up the Nile. In the cool of July, we traveled north to enjoy the charming antique architecture and glorious gardens of Alexandria, and from there we made forays to the azure waters of the Mediterranean. I still can recall, as if it had been but yesterday, our Maxie on the beach, jumping and shrieking with delight as the waves rushed over his pudgy little feet while James and Raoul waded at either side of him with their trousers rolled up, holding his hands.

The post would arrive in intermittent batches, brought from the Ruritanian embassy in a pile to be doled out among us. In addition to the already outdated newspapers, there would be letters for Kitty from Reynard and letters for me from our father and Pontsylvania's mother. Raoul, already well-accustomed to a vicarious Ruritanian life *via* correspondence, exchanged letters with a number of friends in Strelsau and one or two in Constantinople as well as the attorneys and our hopelessly toiling inquiry agents. A condoling letter from Flavia was forwarded to me, the misfortune of Pontsylvania's disappearance having come to her attention. Together we followed and discussed events in Ruritania with interest although everything in the post was old news by the time it arrived.

I will not set down in these pages a narrative of all that transpired in more than two years away from Ruritania. Indeed there is little worthwhile to relate beyond the various more amusing Egyptian anecdotes already shared many times within our family by Raoul. With regard to the matter at hand, my marriage to Gerhard von Plinth, the situation of course remained unchanged. I was a duchess living apart from my husband within the European expatriate community of Cairo. The fact of my husband's whereabouts being unknown was all too shaming to mention and was never discussed. I relied mainly on Raoul, Kitty and James for companionship. Although I did find acquaintance with a few pleasant women, I adroitly avoided the attentions of the occasional gentleman who would take notice of me. My intimidating rank of duchess aided and protected me in this avoidance. I was in retreat, waiting for time to pass.

Through his correspondents Raoul was able to monitor Manfred's activities. Our cousin clearly was not leading anything like a life of retreat though he took no steps in the direction of matrimony. I sometimes fleetingly wished for my own sake that he would do so, but I would then recall he was a murderer; therefore such a wish was all too unkind to any poor girl he might set his sights upon.

Meanwhile the Dowager Duchess Agathe remained in residence and management at Pontsylvania House. Although hers was a fine social and family life in Strelsau, I have no doubt it was a sorrow to her to be kept apart from Max, particularly given the heartache surrounding his missing father. However she was not yet an elderly woman and I expected the opportunity to make it up to her in the future.

In time I did become concerned about Kitty, who was older than I and beyond the age at which most Ruritanian girls would have married. I did not require her to keep herself apart when we received company or went about in public and I encouraged her to dress as finely as she liked. Whenever possible, I would also leave it for her to decide whether or when to disclose she was in my employ. However she had previously known not one word of English, and while at the outset she did have various French idioms commonly in use in Ruritania, her fluency was confined to German and as bright and willing to learn as she was, this put her at a disadvantage. I could see little hope for her forming a suitable connection in Cairo. I recalled also my promise to Reynard to bring her back. As we approached the second anniversary of our arrival I taxed her with these things directly, suggesting she make plans to go home to Eisenstein and to seek a husband. She tossed her head and laughed at me, her eyes twinkling, and inquired as to just which ignorant Ruritanian country bumpkin I would recommend she seek out that she might embark on a life of endless dismal toil by his side. I reasonably protested there were surely better possibilities for her in Ruritania than what she was describing. She conceded this might perhaps be true but said she would not for all the world miss the adventure she was having and that Ruritania, although inevitable at some point, could continue waiting as far as she was concerned. It was no doubt selfish of me and I took pains to conceal it, but I could not help feeling a secret relief in knowing she was not yet ready to leave me.

Our days were bright and filled with pleasures, camaraderie, and endless new discoveries. From the rising of the sun until the parting of our little company at the end of each evening, Ruritania seemed to me diminished and remote while the terrible events which had driven me from my home were as the nightmares of a previous slumber, still in memory yet without substance. But in the nights as I lay alone in darkness waiting for sleep, whether upon a brass bedstead in a hotel room in Alexandria, a cabin bunk in a gently swaying boat upon the Nile or the vast cushioned divan in my Cairo apartments, my thoughts would ever return to Eisenstein. I knew it must be that place which would one day become real again while these days in Egypt would be the dream remembered. Often I wondered what would remain for me when I returned and what might be forever altered or hopelessly lost. Yet as often would I remind myself that although my decisions had taken me down such a ruinous path, I had never meant to bring hurt upon anyone. Many nights I wept, but each morning the sun rose again.

XX. Return to Ruritania ⚜ The passing of the King

There came at last that certain afternoon when we were lounging in basket chairs in the shade of the orange tree, sharing in the gleanings of a recently delivered post. Save for Max we were all taking coffee, which I had learned to love in Egypt, forsaking tea for the rest of my life. James, who of course received his mail separately from the rest of us in the British Legation post bag, was playing a game of hoopla with Max in a thoroughly silly and raucous manner. Raoul sat with his chair tilted back on two legs, one ankle across the other knee, smoking a cigarette, a letter in hand. "Oh ho!" he said, grinning. "Fritz von Tarlenheim writes to me of our cousin Manfred's progress. His lady who entertains upon the trapeze has thrown him over. He is now in pursuit of her replacement, a baroness whose name shall not be herein disclosed, living in estrangement from her husband. He loses embarrassing sums at cards and is seen to be regularly drinking to excess. Fritz is deeply disapproving and concerned. He's such an innocent, is Fritz. I do love Fritz."

A thin and narrow envelope had been adhering to the back of the open one he carelessly held in his other hand, where it appeared slightly threatened by his cigarette. It came loose and fluttered to the ground. James retrieved it, holding it up by one corner gingerly pinched between thumb and forefinger as if it were something foul. "I observe this to be a telegram," he said. "Telegrams are never good; therefore I am grateful it is not mine." He passed it to Raoul.

We all watched in expectant silence. Raoul tore an end off the envelope and withdrew the slip of paper inside. His face was a blank save for a grim tightening about the mouth. He turned his eyes immediately to James while holding the telegram out to me. It was from Pontsylvania's attorney and dated three days prior. "REGRET DD PONTSYLVANIA AGATHE DECEASED YESTERDAY STOP IMMEDIATE RETURN ADVISED STOP RSVP STOP HAUER"

I said, "Oh, no, no! Poor Madame Agathe; what a terrible shame, and how very surprising! I have just now been reading this letter from her in which she states she is in fine health. I wonder what on earth can have happened to her. And now what must we do?"

Raoul replied, "Exactly as Hauer recommends. We must go back, for Maxie's sake. Gerhard's brothers will be as vultures circling above Pontsylvania House. Or perhaps just over the National Bank of Ruritania."

I awoke very late that night to the sound of distant shouting. Stepping out onto my balcony, I saw that a single lamp remained burning within Raoul's apartments. After a few moments of puzzlement, I understood I was overhearing a row between Raoul and James, who had never spoken a harsh word to one another in my presence. I could not make out what was being said but by the tenor of their voices, I perceived one of them was in a terrible rage while the other voice, though also raised and intense, had more of a quality of entreaty. As I continued to listen with bated breath, I became convinced the raging voice was James. I thought I discerned the words "again" and "me" repeated several times but I could get nothing of the meaning of it.

The altercation ceased abruptly. In the deeply shadowed garden below, I saw James pass through a shaft of moonlight, walking swiftly to the front gate. After he had gone out I remained quite some time and pondered, gazing down through ornately wrought iron railings at Raoul's window where the lonely lamp still burned. All was quiet save for the murmur of the fountain and the soft purring of doves. I wanted to go to him yet I dared not, and so at last I went back to bed.

On arrival at Trieste, where we would commence the overland leg of our journey home, we were met with shocking news. King Rudolph V of Ruritania had been assassinated on the very day of our embarkation from Alexandria. It was said there had been two attempts upon his life within the same week. The first by Rupert von Hentzau, who had returned in secret to Strelsau, lured the King to a private meeting and attacked him. They had engaged in a fight to the death and it was Hentzau who had perished. The second attack was carried out by a political extremist who had infiltrated the grounds of the Royal Palace after dark, surprised the King outdoors on a terrace, and shot him. An officer of the Royal Guard had slain the assassin immediately following the fatal shot, and in so doing had saved the lives of others present, including the Queen.

Thus the line of succession of the Elphbergs in Ruritania was broken. Flavia of Gothe-Saxeberg and Elphberg now sat alone as Ruritanian head of state. Although her father held the throne of Gothe-Saxeberg and her mother, Maria Viktoria Elphberg and von Turmen, was Rudolph's aunt, her position appeared precarious, for Ruritania was without an heir apparent. Flavia was fortunate in being surrounded by a supportive cabinet as well as enjoying the strong loyalty of the military. We discussed it in the train.

"She shall have to marry again as soon as is decent," Raoul said. "Someone of The Blood who will be acceptable to the people. I can't think who. They shall have to search high and low. Some of these Royals just don't do enough legitimate procreating, you know. Possibly because they don't necessarily like each other all that much. Now, this tale about Rupert von Hentzau does have me perplexed. Why on earth would Hentzau wish to kill the King? On the contrary, I should think he would have been desperate to win back the favor of the Court so he could come home and get his lands and rents back. And beyond that, I absolutely cannot imagine Rudolph Elphberg besting Hentzau in a fight. No, seriously; that story has a distinct malodor."

At Pontsylvania House, we found my husband's younger brothers all in residence along with their wives and children. The Dowager Duchess Agathe had been laid to rest a week past. We were informed she had mercifully passed away within three days after a sudden and devastating stroke. I thanked the Plinths most humbly for managing all of it without me. The brothers took the opportunity to draw Raoul into conference and question him in minute detail about our efforts to locate Pontsylvania, as well as expounding their various theories about his fate. Mr. Hauer came to the house and conferred first privately with Raoul and then with all of them.

While the gentlemen were in conference, I wrote to Flavia a letter of condolence penned upon the crested stationery of the Duchy of Pontsylvania. It was particularly difficult to compose for I had not admired her husband and I virtually assumed she was of the same mind. I also wondered whether she would ever even look upon my letter with her own eyes or merely see the fact of its receipt upon some list. Surely there were sacks of such letters arriving at the Royal Palace from all over the world. Yet I chose my words sincerely and with care in hopes they might actually come into her hand.

By the time all the Plinths had finally done the decent thing and packed up and taken themselves off, Raoul appeared drawn and exhausted though he made no complaint. We were all deeply fatigued. At last left to ourselves, we slept.

Once recovered, we went to call on our father only to find he was not in Strelsau. In fact he had not been in Strelsau for several weeks. The telegram sent to inform him of our return had been forwarded through the post and we had no way of knowing whether he had yet received it. As in many a past year, he had gone to spend the harvest season at Eisenstein.

There was no discussion of whether or not I would go back. From the day we boarded ship at Alexandria, I had known my ultimate destination.

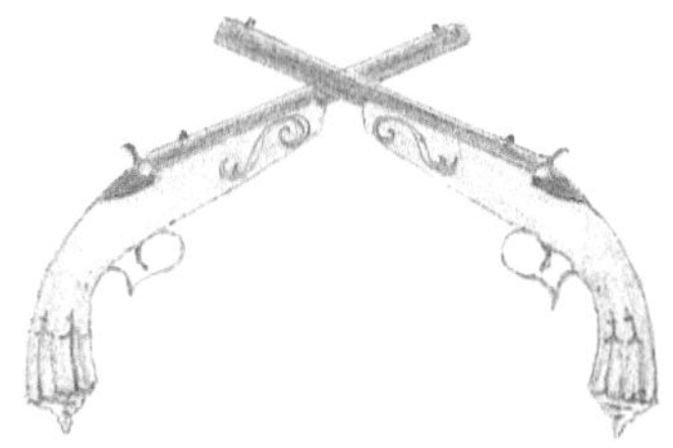

XXI. Love and death at Eisenstein

At Eisenstein, our dear father was completely surprised at our arrival and overjoyed to have us all together, Raoul and I, and Max. Kitty asked for Reynard. He was not in the house but expected to return that night. We all sat down to a long and boisterous supper after which we discussed sleeping arrangements. I settled Max in a bedroom next door to the one in which Kitty was unpacking her trunk. Such a long day had it been, the very moment his sweet head lay upon the pillow and before I had placed my kiss upon his forehead, he was off to sleep.

I ascended alone to my tower where a small window in the dressing room gave a view down over the long hillside behind the house to the rambling line of the stables far below. It was a fine, clear night, the full harvest moon flooding all Eisenstein in a sharply shadowed blue light. I considered I might sit by that window and continue watching, but I could not sit. I changed clothes, switched my shoes for boots and donned a well-worn skirted coat of green velvet.

I went to Kitty's room with my saddle bag in hand and told her I meant to go out for a ride down to the Zenda bridge and back. She protested I should not go alone. I assured her I would be quite safe, and so I went.

For a short while I was young again, galloping full tilt down that old familiar stretch of road in the moonlight. I wore no hat and as my hair began to fall loose, I shook it out and let the long mass of curls fly. I was sixteen, too young yet to marry and my future lying all ahead of me, unknown. I was full of hope and fire, with a wild wind in my face. Such was the strange magic of the night, of the moon, and of Eisenstein.

But finally the moon went down, drifting lower behind the trees until I was left with only the stars, and I turned back.

On entering the lane at the bottom of the hill, I saw a point of light in the stables. Upon my departure the groom assisting me had gone in for the night and we had left no flame to burn there unattended. I urged my horse forward, bringing the pace back up to a trot. It did occur to me momentarily my appearance was in some disarray but this was a concern I had no patience for, and so I dismissed the thought. Dismounting, I tethered the horse and went in.

A lantern had been lit and was hanging from a beam. At the edge of the circle of illumination it cast, Reynard was seated on a keg. He was gazing down at a diminutive volume, bound in red leather, which he held in his hand unopened. He rose promptly as I crossed the threshold, then tucked the little book away into some pocket within the breast of his jacket, not in the haste of concealment but with deliberation. "Welcome to Eisenstein, Your Grace."

Stepping forward into the light, I said, "Do please call me by my name."

"Welcome to Eisenstein, Hilda Marie von Eisen."

"Will you please tell me, Reynard, what has happened while I have been away?"

Softening the words with his little crooked smile, he replied, "Certainly. I will tell you everything. Since last I saw you, there have been nine hundred thirty one sunrises and nine hundred thirty two sunsets. If you wish to know exactly how many lambs, calves and piglets have been born, I will have to consult my books."

"Is there anything else?"

"Yes. Muffin has passed away at the end of a long and noble life. I have buried her with honors and marked the place with a stone which I will show you."

"Is there anything else?"

"Henriette has been made a very happy wife."

"Oh! She has?"

"Yes; did you not know she married?"

"I did not know."

"She is now Madame Dreska. You'll recall her husband, Armand Dreska the younger who took over his father's millinery shop in the village at Zenda. She works there with him now and her creations are highly popular with the ladies. They first became acquainted during her stay here at Eisenstein. I encouraged her actually, as I've known him all my life and he's a very fine fellow. As for herself, she tells me she fell in love by their third encounter, or perhaps I should say, by her third new hat. After you departed to Egypt she found a position in Zenda, to be near him. I'm happy to say he understood why she might have done this and rose to the occasion handsomely."

Dear and loyal Henriette! I recalled her silent, secretive tears on the train and knew myself for a fool. "I must have a new hat soon myself then," I said. "for I shall be very pleased to see her again. Is there anything else?"

"No, there is not. That is all. I am just exactly as you left me, Hilda."

He was indeed as I had left him, for he stood with as dignified a carriage as any gentleman, with that same inquisitive tilt of his head and his blue eyes steadily holding my gaze. A deep stillness fell between us and as silent moments passed, I felt the beating of my own heart. I knew he was again waiting; waiting as always upon me, Hilda Marie von Eisen and von Plinth, Her Grace, the Duchess of Pontsylvania. For my own part, I felt as one about to step forth from some treacherous precipice into a vast emptiness, or perhaps as standing blindfold at the end of a plank in a pirate's tale, yet for so very long had I myself been waiting, there upon the edge of my doom, I was ready at last to give over and to fall.

"Reynard," I said, "In every one of those many nights since last we met, you have been in my thoughts." I held out my arms to him.

He crossed the space between us in an instant and the intense fervency with which he embraced me spoke the answer to the question I had never dared to ask. His loden jacket smelled of pipe tobacco and wood smoke, of horses and hay, of home. With his face hidden in the wild nest of my hair, he asked, "And what has happened with you then, Hildie, over all those many days?"

"I've had a marvelous adventure with Raoul and Kitty and Max. Now it is finished."

"I hope you will tell me all about it.

"I certainly shall. I will tell you everything. Oh, Reynard!" I stood up on my toes and his arms clasped firmly about my waist bore me up. For the sweetest moment and ever so softly, our lips met.

He took me by the shoulders then and gently held me back. "Listen to me, Hilda. You have only just come home after so long a time away. Emotions run high in such a circumstance. I would be deeply grieved if anything should happen that you later regret."

This time it was my eyes that filled with tears.

"Oh Hilda, Hilda! Do not mistake my meaning. I have waited all this time to see you again. I am at your disposal. I will be here tomorrow, and the next day, and the day after that."

"Will you ride with me tomorrow, then?"

"I shall be most pleased to ride with you tomorrow and any other day you wish. Now, may I see to your horse?"

I put my hand to his cheek. He had not shaved that day and probably not the day before. "At what time did you ride out to your work this morning?"

"Oh, before dawn."

"Do go in and sleep, then, and let me take care of the horse myself as I had been already intending to do."

"Thank you, Hilda. May God bless you and keep you. Until tomorrow."

"Until tomorrow, Reynard."

He took up my hands and held them lightly between his own for a moment, then lifted each one in turn to kiss the palm. Saying nothing more, he released me and quickly went out.

I found my hands were trembling as I went to retrieve the horse. I went through the motions of removing saddle bag, saddle, and blanket. I backed her into her box, brushed her coat, freed her of her bridle. There was a basket of apples on the shelf as usual. I gave her one, and stroked her face and praised her. Dragging over an oaken box for a step stool, I extinguished the lantern. Such was the tumult in my heart, I wondered how I would ever sleep at all that night. Reaching for my saddle bag, I turned to go.

There was the figure of a man before me, occupying the doorway through which I had meant to pass, a slender black silhouette without a face. I did not need to see the face. Recognition was immediate. In mocking tones, he said, "Welcome to Eisenstein, Hilda Marie von Eisen."

I was paralyzed in that moment, stunned with a cold shock like an instant freezing of the blood throughout my body. I conceived the fear that should he come towards me or try to touch me, I'd not be able to move.

He remained there blocking the doorway for what

seemed an agonizingly long time. Presumably he awaited my reply but I could muster no words. At last he spoke again. "It has been said by many I am a very handsome and cultured gentleman. Yet this is your preference, Hilda. Manx, your common lackey, dirty from head to foot from his long day's toil, who romances you in the stable while these beasts look on. In future I expect we shall see you slinking into the house following your equestrian expeditions with your skirt soiled and bits of hay in your hair. Do you not worry, though, about the family von Plinth? Will they have their little Duke raised by a woman who lies lower than some *demimondaine*?

"I know everything about you, Hilda. I know, for example, that you have in your possession the ring, the seal of Pontsylvania, which you took from Gerhard's cold, dead hand. I also know of another ring with an emerald stone which Manx keeps in his bedside table, wrapped in a dainty handkerchief bearing your initials."

This last astonishing statement instantly jolted me free from my state of paralysis. I said, "He does?"

"You know it."

"In truth I knew no such thing. But who here at Eisenstein do you pay to go rifling through people's bureau drawers for you?"

"I do not pay anyone."

"Oh, of course, you don't have to pay. Your loyal mother has been your assistant."

"There is only one thing I do not know about you, Hilda. Do you care; have you ever cared in the slightest for one single moment, about what you have done to me? You are my absolute ruin. I am damned for you. I gave up my immortal soul to set you free from that overstuffed prig Pontsylvania whom we both know that you despised. What more could any man ever do for the sake of a woman, Hilda, than what I have done for you? Answer me, Hilda."

"I have no answer."

"You are the only woman I have ever loved, will ever love, could ever love."

"You do not love me, Manfred."

"Oh, perhaps you misunderstand. I did not mean to say that I love you now. I have learned to hate you, Hilda. I hate you absolutely and completely. With every step and every breath, day and night, waking and sleeping, I hate you. Nothing would give me more pleasure than to see you dead, unless perhaps I might see you crawl on your knees before me in the dirt and beg . . . and then see you dead."

If one passed down through the stables to the farthest end from where I stood, there was an exit debouching into a yard from which a bridle trail led down through a beech copse and ultimately out into the open park. I turned and bolted for it in the dark. I did trip but once over some unidentifiable item of clattering barn paraphernalia and was thrown to my knees, but got myself up again immediately and raced on. Gaining the door, I threw it open and ran out under the stars. He had moved just as quickly and was rounding the corner of the building as I emerged. Running desperately, I was barely ahead of him. He shouted, "Hilda, STOP!" There was such sharp tone of menace in his voice, I did stop for an instant, whirling to look at him and then quickly retreating backward as he advanced upon me, matching my pace. He had drawn out a small pocket pistol and held it forth at arm's length. His hand was violently shaking, whether from anxiety at the boldness of his own actions or the intensity of his rage, I could not tell. The little gun wavered, threatening my face, my chest, my throat. Slowly, he drew closer as I continued to back away.

I had managed by then to get a hand inside the saddle bag. It slipped from my fingers and fell, leaving only a cocked pistol in my grasp. In the extremity of my haste, I made no effort at taking aim. I simply pointed in his direction and fired.

He was thrown off his feet. Sitting on the ground with splayed legs, he clapped his free hand to the side of his white cravat from which a dark stain then spread with such shocking rapidity, the hopelessness of his situation was immediately apparent. Although he still held the pocket pistol out before him, it slid from his loosening grip and fell away, leaving an empty hand with which he reached out to me in a gesture of entreaty. For an utterly horrifying moment I heard him struggling for breath. Then came an even more terrible silence as his arms dropped and he fell back. Under the light of the stars, I could see the faint gleam of his open eyes.

I rushed back into the stables and cast about for a place to put down the hot, fouled pistol. There was an iron stove, used but occasionally in the winter months. I dropped the pistol there, then picked up my skirts and flew for the house, up the long slope with my heart hammering.

I stumbled into the back hallway and leaned against the wall. A man was speaking somewhere nearby. It was Raoul's voice, coming from the back parlor. I went in. Reynard and Raoul were leaning companionably against the mantlepiece, gazing down into the fire in a mirrored pose, each with one boot up on the fender. Their difference in stature was striking in that setting, Reynard being the taller of the two. They turned their curly heads, one ruddy and one dark, to look at me. "Ah, Hilda," said Raoul. "See here, I have found Reynard and we are having a philosophical discussion about the moral conventions of European society. This despite the fact Reynard should be in bed, but the topic is of pressing interest."

"I need help," I gasped. "I have shot Manfred."

"Manfred! Oh, for God's sake. Is he here?"

"Klench has been rarely seen at Eisenstein since your departure," said Reynard. "At present I'd hazard it's over a year since the last time. His mother complains of it."

"He is here now," I said. "He has followed me from Strelsau. He meant to shoot me and so . . . I shot him first."

Raoul was still perhaps not taking the matter quite seriously enough. "Well I hope that you have killed him then, for the man is a pestilence."

"But I believe I have indeed killed him," I said. "I did not intend to but my aim was wild. It's terrible but I had to stop him and there wasn't a second to spare."

Reynard said, "You mean this." This was not a query but a statement.

"Good God," said Raoul.

Reynard took my arm to steady me as we raced back down the slope, slipping and sliding. At the bottom of the hill he released his hold and from there we all ran, though I was certain in my heart there was no use in all this rush beyond making the proper display of effort. Arriving at Manfred's side, Raoul gazed down on him for a moment, drew in a deep breath and slowly let it out, then squatted cautiously so as to avoid bloodying his trousers. He lifted up a limp arm and laid his fingers across the wrist. Next dropping the arm with a muttered oath, he pressed his hand directly upon the drenched breast of Manfred's shirt.

"You see," I said. "God help me, I really have killed him."

"Yes, Hilda, indeed you have. It's entirely his own fault, of course. Would that he had been more direct and simply shot himself without obliging you to do it. But as I've mentioned a number of times before, he has ever been a sniveling coward." Raoul produced a handkerchief and hastily cleaned the blood from his hand as best he could. Following upon this, he took up the pocket pistol and examined it closely. He jerked back his head in surprise. "Oh, for God's sake, Manfred! Even in dying, an unmitigated ass!"

"Why," I cried, "What is it?"

Raoul stood up, held forth the little gun and pulled the trigger. With a clicking sound, a hinged panel on the top flew open and a tongue of flame shot straight upwards from the aperture.

I was aghast. "What is this thing?"

Raoul pressed the little door forward with his thumb; it snapped shut and the flame was extinguished. "A device for lighting cigars. It contains a liquid fuel. Naphtha, I believe. It has a wick, like a tiny oil lamp. Pulling the trigger opens the outlet for the flame while at the same time striking a spark which lights the wick. It's perfectly mad. One carries around in one's pocket a little flask full of volatile flammable liquid, designed to create sparks and flame, appearing to be some sort of derringer with a barrel you can point at people and a trigger you can pull. Who on earth thinks of these things? This is the very latest gentleman's toy, from Austria. I had heard about them but I'd not seen one yet."

"But he was pursuing me with that in his hand and pointing it at me! That after raving about how I have utterly destroyed him, and his hatred of me, and wishing to see me dead. I thought he meant to shoot me!"

"Well, he was not going to shoot you with this. I suppose he might just conceivably have intended a murder by immolation but considering how you are dressed, carrying that off would seem to require getting down on his knees and holding your skirt hems to the flame with your kind cooperation. I should think more likely he meant you to believe it a real pistol for the purpose of terrorizing you which, if that were his intent, worked exceedingly well. In any event, this idiotic miscalculation may well represent the boldest deed of action ever undertaken in his miserable craven life. Assuming of course we don't count throwing an adorable little dog off a tower.”

Reynard stood behind me, laying gentle hands upon my shoulders. “It will be all right, Hilda,” he said, “It will be all right.”

Pulling away from him, I exclaimed, “But now, along with everything else I have done, I am a murderer!”

“No, no, no, Hilda. You are not.”

“Do you honestly imagine any magistrate is going to accept that having met my own cousin in a place where he had every right to be, I felt compelled to shoot him through the neck because he showed me this ridiculous toy pistol?”

There was a horrified silence, ultimately broken by Raoul. “I must admit you have a point. Your position does appear uncertain. There will be no little amount of awkwardness in trying to explain just what led up to all this. I worry especially about Aunt Olympia and what she will say against you. She might swear to anything. The poor woman will be as an avenging harpy.”

“Consider also,” I said, “that my husband mysteriously vanished and is thought likely to have met with foul play. No suspicion in that matter has ever been turned upon me, but once it becomes known I am in the way of shooting the men in my family, will that not change?”

Reynard said, “It cannot happen. It absolutely must not happen. I will say I killed him. It will be for the best. Think of Max.”

Raoul turned to him. “Oh, Reynard! Oh, most excellent Reynard, you cannot have killed him.”

“Of course I can!”

“No, no, you cannot, because you are common, if you

will kindly forgive me saying so. Only a gentleman may kill another gentleman. Hilda, I recall you carry a brace of pistols?"

"Yes, they are the set you gave me."

"Where is the one you fired?"

"In the stable on top of the stove."

"And the other?"

"In my saddle bag." I turned and pointed to the spot where it still lay upon the ground. "There."

"Is it loaded?"

"Yes. I always ride with both of them loaded."

"Excellent. How perfectly convenient. Now I want you to get it out and shoot me with it." He walked a few steps away and took up a position. "I should be standing right about here, I think"

"What?"

Raoul was hastily getting off his jacket, which he tossed aside upon a bush. "I just want you to pink me a bit. Then Reynard will ride post-haste to get the magistrate out of bed and report he has just been compelled, by my order, to referee a duel emerging from my final loss of temper over Manfred von Eisen Klench's interminable insulting pestering of my sister. I am so sorry, Reynard; I know you are very tired. Come, Hilda, you are an excellent shot and you need not stand very far away. I know you can do it. Or if you really don't want to, Reynard can do it. He is, as I mentioned, extremely tired. But we must get on with it."

I continued to protest. "But this would not be a legal duel! With no physician here and only Reynard as a witness? That is, unless you think to include me, a woman and the very subject of the conflict, though at least I did not count out your paces for you and drop the handkerchief. Really, it is hard to know which witness may be found less acceptable than the other. You will never get away with it!"

"You are right, Hilda. I will not get away with it. But they'll not hang me. I will not spend one day in a cell nor will they clap me in shackles as they surely would Reynard. They will accept my parole and then bleed me of some money and take away my posting. I assure you there is plenty of precedent. The honorable gentlemen of the peerage are often shooting and stabbing one another in our polite Ruritanian society."

"But you will be disgraced; you could be sent away!"

"Well then I will just have to remove myself to some God-forsaken place. Cairo, for example. Quickly now; I am ready."

And so it was that having just shot my cousin, I proceeded to shoot my brother as well. The bullet creased his upper arm quite deeply, tearing a bloody rent in his sleeve. With his opposite hand, he took the pistol away from me and dropped it by Manfred's feet. He passed Manfred's cigar lighter to Reynard, who pocketed it. His sleeve was soaked. Thin streams of blood began to course down over his hand and drip from his fingertips. He said, "We must compare notes about exactly how this unfortunate thing has occurred. As soon as you revive me, for I believe I'm about to faint."

While trudging back up the hill path yet again, I met a man walking down with a lantern in one hand and a breeched shotgun in the other. It was our head gamekeeper, who had evidently been already to bed as his shirt was outside his breeches and his vest not buttoned. "Good evening, Your Grace," he said to me, "We must have poachers in the park tonight. I swear I have heard shooting."

"It is not poachers, Mr. Ricard. There has been a duel of honor with pistols, out behind the stables, between my brother and Mr. Klench."

"Indeed, a duel? Oh, Madam! I do hope Mr. Raoul is not hurt."

XXII. Gentlemen's justice ❧ Revelations from my father

The only person who did any more sleeping in the Eisenstein manor house that night was Max. Following the application of bandages, brandy and a clean shirt, Raoul apologized on his knees to poor Aunt Olympia, who sobbed and screamed until she was dragged back to her bed and the doctor sent for. Raoul also apologized standing up to our father, who assured him there was no need in a discreetly lowered voice. Our father, after all, had come of an earlier generation for which the settling of a grievance by means of a fair fight agreed upon between two young gentlemen, despite the risks, was virtually assumed a sort of inevitable misfortune.

Shortly after dawn, the magistrate and a pair of bailiffs from Zenda arrived with Reynard, who had never slept at all. After some deliberation, the bailiffs were charged with escorting Reynard and Raoul back to Zenda where they would all board the train for Strelsau.

I soon fell miserably ill for a fortnight, most of which I spent in bed.

The Honorable Manfred von Eisen Klench, a bachelor not yet thirty years of age, was solemnly laid to rest in the churchyard at Eisenstein. I was not well enough to appear at the service, though I was to hear it drew a gathering of considerable size. Our staff from the house attended, I suspect largely out of respect for my father, while a number of relations traveled from their various dwelling places around the countryside. A contingent of Manfred's associates from Strelsau entrained for Zenda together and shared hired coaches to convey them across the river to the church. The grim circumstances of his untimely passing had evidently created something of a sensation.

From my sharp-eyed Kitty, I heard of a tall, slender and elegant woman dressed in full mourning, her face and hair deeply obscured within a large veil of heavy lace draped over a wide-brimmed hat, who arrived unescorted and sat at the back of the church. She departed immediately after the service to sequester herself inside her private coach, from which she observed the graveside prayers and lowering of the casket at a distance. When the mourners began to disperse, she was promptly driven away, having spoken to no one. I assumed this lady to be Manfred's baroness of the unfortunate marriage. I felt much sympathy for her, yet at the same time I was sure I had inadvertently spared her from far greater misfortunes.

In the following days, a fine white marble monument

was placed. It bears above Manfred's name the arched inscription "Seek Me in Heaven," and beneath his life dates the legend, "Perished in a Duel of Honor." Or so I was told, for although I have been countless times to the church over the years hence, and even walked among the graves on several sorrowful occasions, I have never looked at it.

In time, I would come to know that Raoul and Reynard were taken to the Eisenstein town house where an officer of the Royal Guard was billeted on them to observe Raoul's parole. Ten days on, my father joined them there after installing Aunt Olympia, at his own expense, in the most luxurious hotel in Strelsau where she would reside until her relocation to Biarritz. Proceedings regarding the determination of Raoul's fate were considerably delayed due to the funerary observances for the King, which stretched out for many more days. In consequence of this, Raoul, Reynard, my father and the guardsman all greatly increased their skills at four handed whist.

When at last they returned to Eisenstein, Raoul had been permitted one week's leave to spend with us following which he was required to remove himself promptly from Ruritania. After remaining outside the country for a minimum of three years he would be eligible to be recalled by Royal decree, assuming of course he had done nothing further to tarnish his character. In addition to this, Aunt Olympia was to be paid a compensatory pension. Raoul having also been relieved of his posting, this would fall for some time at least upon the Eisenstein estate.

The guardsman accompanied Raoul and Reynard back

to Eisenstein to remain with my brother for the final week of his parole. He was then to escort Raoul on the train to Trieste and see him board ship. He was a great strapping young man with a magnificent moustache, by the name of Bernenstein. On being introduced to me, he conveyed the Queen's compliments, disclosing she had personally assigned him so as to ensure my brother's respectful treatment. It was very kind of Flavia.

During that week, my father and Max and I spent every possible moment with Raoul. The four handed whist tournament also continued nightly with a great deal of jollity. All was bittersweet.

When the end came, I accompanied my brother to his room after breakfast. I sat on the bed and watched as he completed packing up his things. I fell into tears. He sat down beside me and took me in his arms. "Oh, Hildie, Hildie, Hildie."

"I am like a Jonah, bringing down ruin upon everyone around me."

"Oh, nonsense, Hilda, I am not ruined; only set back a bit. And we will all miss each other very much, you and Papa and Maxie and me, but we were always going to have to anyway. I would not have stayed. And Hildie, you do not understand, my dear, sweet girl, how very much I owe to you. All the diamonds and pearls and rubies in Christendom could never pay my debt to you."

"For what?"

"Why, for having married and for making a Maxie. For giving Eisenstein an heir."

"Were you not intending to?"

"I really, really do not want to, Hilda, and may God forgive me. The very thought of having to engage in the marital relationship makes me positively ill. You see, the truth is, I only want to live with James. There, that's it, you see; I want to be with James, and you can add that to our list of unmentionable matters which is getting awfully long. I only pray that he will have me back. And that reminds me now to search my pockets and make sure I've got rid of all my cigarettes. It's going to make for a miserable journey, but Bernenstein does not smoke, so that being the case I think I will manage it. It is my offering, you see, for James always hated putting up with my smoking." With a grin and a twinkling eye, he added, "Not to mention as I now crawl back to prostrate myself at his gate in sackcloth and ashes, disgraced by my evidently superlative marksmanship and without a post, I can hardly expect him to buy me tobacco when I find myself depleted in funds."

Softly, I asked, "Was James ever in Constantinople?"

"It was there we first met. When he was honored with a promotion and reassigned to the Egyptian Legation, an unexpected and awful misfortune brought about by his foolish displays of exceptional competence, he was quite distraught and prepared to resign but his people in England are aged and not well off. I would not be the object of such a terrible choice on his part, so I dissuaded him. I secured a transfer to Cairo for myself, though it took quite some time and it was a bit harrowing, the uncertainty and the waiting."

"And then I took you away. Not only once, but twice."

"Hilda, you were my darling little sister long before I ever went to Constantinople and that does not change. James cannot entirely understand. He was raised an only child, poor boy. But do not worry. I am hopeful and whatever happens, I do assure you, I shall make my way."

Taking my hands in his, he went on, "Now with regard to you, dear girl. As I believe I have mentioned from time to time, it's a horrible world. We are every one of us prisoners, born into our respective cells. But let me impart to you a most valuable lesson I learned from James. I beg you to heed it. It is possible to climb over the walls, or tunnel under, or get around some way. You need not give up all your happiness.

"James was not the first I ever admired so very much in my life, Hilda Dear. He was the second. But the first was never meant for me. He is all for you. Consider Reynard. He is the best, the very best. There is not a man among all your kings and princes, your dukes and barons and honorable gentlemen, who can hold a candle to our Reynard. And I will tell you now what he has never yet been able to say. He worships the very air you breath and the ground on which you tread. Do consider Reynard, Hilda."

I protested, "Oh, I quite agree with you about Reynard as I suppose you somehow already know, but how can it possibly be managed? My husband has gone forever yet still I remain a married woman."

"I don't know how you will do it but do not run from

it. You and Reynard must confer. You may sail to Canada and assume false names while he grows an imperial. Or you may sneak about after dark and never speak of it. Remember, nobody here is against you now. Manfred has greatly elevated his reputation by dying bravely in a duel and Auntie O is taking herself off to foreign parts. There's not one person left here who does not adore you, Hilda. Both you and Reynard command the loyalty of all Eisenstein."

"But what about Papa?"

"He may surprise you. Do give him a chance. He has always been on my side without fail and look what a bad son I am."

After Lieutenant Bernenstein and Raoul had gone, I went for a stroll in the park with our dear father. Arm in arm, we walked the path that follows down along the line of ancient oaks to the little stone bridge, where we would linger for a time and watch for trout in the brook before turning back.

"I am so sorry, Papa," I said, "that you have to pay Auntie O. It is most unfair."

"Oh, I do not mind, Hildie," he replied, "It comes out in the wash, as they say. I am no further behind than before."

"Why, how is that?"

"Ah, well, truth be told, Manfred had been bleeding me at an even greater rate and I had got almost accustomed to the outlay."

"Bleeding you? Why Papa, do you mean to say he was blackmailing you?"

"I supposed that is a fairly accurate term. It is not that I have committed any dark deeds in my quite pedestrian life. It was about your brother. Manfred insinuated to me he was often on the verge of openly denouncing Raoul over certain private aspects of his character. He did not claim to possess a damning letter or anything of that nature, yet I suspected what he claimed to know was essentially the truth and so it was a threat I took quite seriously. He first made mention of it to me upon the announcement of your engagement to Pontsylvania and then on the day of your wedding he alluded to it again. Soon thereafter commenced a series of occasional requests to borrow sums of money which he made no effort to repay. You see, Hildie, he had asked my blessing regarding your hand in marriage on the day following your seventeenth birthday and then again exactly one year later. On both occasions I felt it too soon for you to be obliged to reply to any proposal and so I twice declined on that basis to give an answer."

"But had you agreed, Papa, I could still have refused him."

"Oh, in principle you could, but at such an age, with the understanding you were going against my wishes added to the prospect of enduring the dreadful awkwardness of thus rebuking your cousin and disappointing your aunt, I believe you would have found it more than difficult to know your own true inclination."

"Yes, Papa, I suppose you are right."

"So I thought, and therefore I would not have it put upon you. I did hold great hopes for Manfred in those days and wished you might come to find more worth in him in maturity than you had in childhood. Nevertheless I believed you too young yet to be forced to a decision and I required him to either wait or turn elsewhere, and so I have no doubt he was deeply disappointed when I ultimately bestowed my favor on Gerhard von Plinth. On his first request to borrow, he implied I could well afford to lend what could only be a minute portion of some grand amount he presumed Pontsylvania to have settled upon me directly. Pontsylvania had indeed most generously funded several improvements here on our estate which have been of excellent benefit to us and to our tenancy, but of course I received not a *pfennig* into my own hands from him at any time. Manfred would have it that I'd sold you off for a fat purse as if you were a thoroughbred horse. In truth I was shocked to know such an abhorrent suggestion could pass his lips. I did not even bother to deny it; I could not stoop to such a discussion. I'm sure he meant to cause me regret for having passed him over but the true influence on my thoughts regarding that matter was quite the opposite. Indeed one does learn much of the character of a man by the opportunity of seeing his wishes denied."

"Papa, does Raoul know of this?"

"Oh, no, no. I didn't want to burden him with it. Raoul is a fine man, Hilda; a very fine man, and a son of whom I shall always be extremely proud. But it is a terrible society we live in. To be bright and brave and good is not enough. A man may find himself utterly destroyed over unimportant matters other people really have no business to know or care about. So, all points considered, I really do not think I shall miss Manfred very much and I am happier to pay Olympia. Poor Olympia."

XXIII. The Queen's visit ✤ Flavia imparts a confidence

Later on that very afternoon, a closed and curtained black coach escorted by two dozen mounted guardsmen arrived at the Eisenstein manor house. I had not expected this. I quickly tidied my hair and hastened to the formal drawing room. A tall and stately woman, arrayed in full mourning and heavily veiled, was ushered in.

I curtsied deeply. "You honor our house, Your Majesty."

She lifted and folded back the layers of veils, revealing her face. I had been prepared to see a visage drawn with care and sorrow, but I was surprised. Flavia was radiant. "I am so very pleased to see you, Hilda," she said. "How long it has been."

"Thank you, Your Majesty."

To my complete astonishment, she then said, "I have come to see Mr. Manx."

To my further astonishment, Reynard immediately

entered the room. "I am here," he said. I could see the backs of two guardsmen stationed in the hall who had permitted him to pass. He closed the door.

I felt a brief anxiety lest he not know how to conduct himself in the Royal Presence, but in truth I was the one entirely out of my depth in that moment and all that was to follow. He advanced confidently and went down on one knee before the Queen, his right hand covering his heart. He bowed his head. "Your Majesty."

She offered her right hand. With his left, he raised it to his lips and kissed The Ring bearing the Royal Signet of the Elphbergs. I knew this to be an ancient circular carnelian, carved with a crown between the antlers of a stag's head. It had been re-set to fit Flavia's hand, transferred to a simple gold bezel and accompanied only by two pearls, these placed opposite each other along the axis of her finger. Rudolph's ring had been much larger, with a heavy band and the signet stone set above rows of diamonds.

Flavia said, "Please stand, Mr. Manx."

He rose to his feet but she did not release his hand. And so they stood, hand in hand and face to face, with their fair complexions, their clear blue eyes, their mirrored profiles with the high, straight lines of their noses, his untidy copper curls and hers, neatly tamed by the hands of some skillful lady in waiting. Amazed, I asked myself why I had never seen, but the answer followed immediately upon the question. I had never seen because he was a common man while she was of The Blood; she was the Queen, and never in either my experience or my thoughts had they come anywhere near to one another.

Flavia said, "You know why I wished to see you."

Reynard replied, "Yes, I believe I do."

She said, "I do count Madame von Eisen and von Plinth among my loyal friends, but you may wish to speak privately."

He answered solemnly, "For my part, there is nothing Her Grace the Duchess may not be privy to."

Flavia smiled. "Let us sit down together, then. Please come close to me." She chose for herself a gracefully shaped armchair on which she sat erect in her royal manner. I subsided gratefully onto the settee immediately behind me, for I was feeling weak at the knees. Reynard brought a small side chair and placed himself directly before her.

She said, "You are aware, then, that you are my brother."

"Yes, I am. I did not know of this in my childhood. My stepfather who raised me, Everard Manx, explained my true history to me when I came of age."

"And our father, Axel von Turmen, likewise revealed this to me before I came to Ruritania as the guest of my cousin Rudolph Elphberg whom I was contracted to marry. I wanted very much to speak to you but Rudolph most adamantly would not allow it. Now that I am on my own, it is my decision. I wish to apologize on behalf of the family von Turmen for what happened to your mother. Our father has related to me how he visited the royal chateau at Zenda as a young prince and that he would enjoy a pleasant recreation there in going among the people *incognito*. It was in this way that he met your mother. It is perhaps important to understand my father was the third son of his house and grew up with no expectations regarding the crown of Gothe-Saxeberg. When his elder brothers were killed together in the same tragic incident, his status was drastically altered in an instant. He returned immediately to Gothe-Saxeberg to take up his responsibilities as heir apparent to the throne. It was not until he again came to the royal chateau at Zenda on a state visit several years later that he discovered the fact of your birth. He had in the interim married my mother, who is also Rudolph's aunt, born Princess Maria Elphberg of Ruritania, then Crown Princess Maria Elphberg and von Turmen of Gothe-Saxeberg. And your mother had married Mr. Manx."

"Yes," said Reynard. "That is all as I understand it. My mother and Mr. Manx had been friends from childhood. He married my mother and simply permitted the assumption by all that he was my father. And I hope it may comfort Your Majesty to know my mother never doubted the sincerity of the Prince von Turmen's affection for her. She also felt complete sympathy and understanding with regard to his reasons for leaving Zenda and passing out of her life so suddenly. She expressed all of this to Mr. Manx, who later related it to me. My mother was an extraordinary woman, not only in beauty but in intelligence and compassion. She had no secrets from Mr. Manx and I believe she learned to love him very much."

"Thank you," said Flavia. "I am greatly comforted in this. I cannot help feeling, nonetheless, there should be recompense for the birthright denied to you by that sudden and tragic twist of fate. As you are no doubt aware, Rudolph's mother did not recover from his birth and his younger half brother, Michael Elphberg, was next born of the Old King's second and morganatic marriage. Michael was styled Grand Duke of Strelsau and possessed holdings which included the Royal Chateau at Zenda. Upon his death, the title was vacated and his properties reverted to the Crown. I offer this title and the holdings associated with it to you."

Reynard bowed his head. "Your Majesty, I am more deeply grateful than I can ever say for this so kind and generous offer. However I must entreat that you will forgive me. I cannot accept. Everard Manx was a man of fine character and as good a father to me as any son might ever wish to have. I also loved my mother dearly and I cherish her memory. Notwithstanding that they no longer live, for their honor I must remain simply Reynard Manx."

"Very well. I am truly sorry to hear this but your reasons do you much credit, so I must accept your decision."

Reynard then lifted his eyes to hers. "Thank you, Your Majesty. I do have two requests of you, if you will be so kind as to hear them. I am deeply grateful that you've come to me because I had intended to apply to you after the New Year."

Flavia smiled, and I sensed she was intrigued. "Yes, I

will hear your requests."

Reynard said, "I first would ask to bring your attention to the plight of Her Grace Hilda von Eisen and von Plinth who sits here with us. Her husband the Duke of Pontsylvania rode away from this house over three years ago, having stated his intention to carry out a short business trip to Vienna. Since that day he has never been seen or heard from again. The Duke's brother-in-law, Raoul von Eisen, has directed the most extensive possible inquiries in efforts to locate the Duke. Raoul von Eisen has also thoroughly examined all financial records and found no indication of preparations to abscond or take up an alternate residence. The Duke has made no contact with anyone, in any way. Even upon the death of his mother, with whom he enjoyed a deeply affectionate relationship, he was not heard from. I believe the conclusion is inescapable that he is no longer living and also that the circumstances of his unfortunate fate will remain forever unknown. My request is that the Duke should now be declared deceased, thus investing his son Gerhard Maxim von Plinth with the title Duke of Pontsylvania and advancing Hilda von Plinth to the status of widowhood and the title Dowager Duchess of Pontsylvania. Although I understand it is not generally customary to declare a missing person deceased at such an interval, in these circumstances there would seem to be no reasonable cause for further delay. Not only would it benefit the living if this adjustment could be made, it would make it possible for the Mass for the Dead to be celebrated for the soul of the

Duke and for his memorial to be placed in the Cathedral of Strelsau among those of his ancestors."

Flavia turned her gaze to me for a moment. One would think I might have been ashamed, for it was as if her brilliant blue eyes looked directly into my heart, yet her countenance bore nothing but the kindest understanding and I felt we were in complete accord, she and I. She said, "I am pleased to agree to this request. This is of course not only a matter of law but a matter for the church as well. I count the Archbishop of Strelsau among my closest friends. I shall speak with him."

Reynard replied, "I am profoundly grateful for this, Your Majesty."

"And you have another request?"

"I do, Your Majesty. You have a Lieutenant Bernenstein among your Royal Guards."

"Oh, yes. I have cause for the deepest gratitude to Bernenstein, for he made the most selfless and heroic effort to save the life of the King and although he was not able to do so, it was only through his valiant actions that I and others present remained unharmed and the assassin was prevented from escape."

"My request is that Lieutenant Bernenstein be granted permission to marry."

Flavia laughed in delighted surprise. "Indeed? To marry? And who is the lady Lieutenant Bernenstein would wish to marry?"

"It is my sister, Katerina Manx."

"He has spoken to you?"

"Yes, he has."

"And does your sister agree?"

"Indeed she does, wholeheartedly."

Prior to her departure, Flavia asked me to show her our gardens. While we wandered side by side over the paths; her manner and carriage were not those of the Queen yet rather of an intimate companion. She said, "Of course I understand why you felt the need to leave us for a time, Hilda. The scandal of the Duke's disappearance must have been a such a horror; I can scarcely imagine how it must have been for you. But now I shall have need of every true friend in the days ahead and I am therefore so very glad you've come back. You recall Helga von Strofzin, now von Strofzin and von Tarlenheim?"

"Oh yes, of course. The most lovely lady. Do you think she is happy?"

"With Fritz von Tarlenheim? Oh, of course. They are among the lucky ones. Helga remains my dearest and most devoted Lady in Waiting. When you next return to Strelsau, you must please send word to her that you are in residence."

"Of course, Flavia, and a telegram will bring me in haste at any time you should want me."

"Thank you, Hilda. Now I must ask you about Mr. Manx. Please tell me in all honesty, do you think you know him well enough to say whether I may entirely trust him, not only today but for the future?"

"Oh, Flavia, I have no doubt of that. I have known

Reynard Manx since I was a small girl, I am especially close to his sister Kitty and I knew their father Everard Manx as well. They are the best of people."

"I am very happy to have made his acquaintance at last," she said, "and I hope to see him again. But I do know I would not be invulnerable should he prove to be an unscrupulous man. He did demonstrate much today in refusing my offer, yet it would be possible to develop new ambitions."

"Of unscrupulousness he is incapable by his very nature, and as for ambition, he has no need of it. He already enjoys the charge of a great domain, for he rules with deep devotion over all of this." With a sweep of my arm, I gestured to the rolling fields, farmsteads and forests that fell away beneath us to the foothills and peaks beyond. "I believe he is happy with his lot and wants for nothing."

"Yet he has no wife?"

"Such a man may take a wife whenever he is ready to, I am sure."

Flavia smiled in that impish way I had sometimes seen before. "Ah, no doubt you are right, Hilda."

We walked on in silence for a time until we stopped to admire the magnificent hydrangea trees, which bloom at the end of summer and then transmute their color from creamy white to the deepest of pinks as the nights turn cool. Flavia cradled a great cluster of blossoms in her elegant hands and lifted it to her face, breathing in the sweet scent. I noted she wore a ring on her left hand, a flat gold band bearing no jewel but marked with the tracery of some inscription. "Do you recall our conversation years ago," she asked, "about the privilege of motherhood?"

"Yes, Flavia, I do."

"I know all Ruritania now assumes," she said, "the incumbent Elphberg line has been broken, but they are wrong."

"Oh, Flavia!"

"Yes, Hilda, it is true. My Rudolph, the great love of all my life, has left me with the ultimate gift to comfort me in my sorrow. It is too soon for a public announcement but to you I'm sure I may safely entrust this confidence: At this very moment the heir apparent of Ruritania lives and is resting close to my heart, waiting to join us in the spring."

It will forever remain a mystery to me how a woman of Flavia's intelligence and refinement could conceivably have been in love with Rudolph Elphberg. There are some things in life that simply cannot be accounted for.

XXIV. All secrets revealed

Late that evening, I sat with Reynard in the back parlor, on the settee before the fire. I had drawn the pins from my hair one by one, piling them on his cupped palm until I'd found them all, after which he had slipped them into his pocket. My hand clasped in his and my head leaning against his shoulder, we had long been gazing into the flames in a comfortable silence. I was tired, yet enjoying a deep contentment such as I had not felt since the better moments of my childhood. On the cushioned seat of a chair beside us lay two kittens, a gray and a calico, curled back to back and asleep with that peaceful abandon common to cats and little children.

I said, "I shall have to return to Strelsau. There is much to be done there."

"Do you expect you will be coming back?"

"Of course I shall come back. It is my hope to spend as much of my time here as possible and I thought to put Kitty in charge of Pontsylvania House if she wishes it.

With her husband in the Queen's service, I think she will find it a most convenient residence. But in any event, my future whereabouts need not concern you very much."

"Why does this not concern me?"

"Because I want you to come with me."

"I shall be pleased to escort you."

"No, no, Reynard, I do not mean that I wish to be 'escorted.' I simply want you to come with me. You will not be able to sit at my side in the cathedral when the mass is said for Gerhard von Plinth. On that day I must walk alone, but that need be the only such day."

"Well then I suppose I will have to get some better clothes."

"I'm sure that can be accomplished."

"I had planned for tomorrow a ride across to Zenda, to Lauch Farm, that I might look over a pony I thought possibly to make a purchase of for Max. Do you think there would still be time for that?"

"Oh! Of course there shall be time for a venture of such extraordinary importance. May I accompany you? Just for the pleasure; when it comes to the pony, I do promise not to interfere."

"Certainly you may come, Hilda, and you may interfere about the pony as well, should you wish to." There was an interval of hesitation then, and finally he sighed. "And I suppose it is now time that I should tell you all my secrets."

"Your secrets? Dear God, have you more secrets? What else can there possibly be beyond what I have already heard this day?"

"I will tell you everything. On the day you were married, I walked alone up to the castle on Wachterberg. I sat up on the parapet for some three hours or so and contemplated throwing myself off."

"Oh, Reynard!"

"It was not that I had ever had any expectations of you, of course, but somehow the reality and immediacy of your marriage had cast me down into the blackest despondency. However in the end, I thought of my father and my sister, and I climbed down and went back home. I never slept at all that night, both imagining and trying not to imagine you in the arms of that man. It would have been easier to bear if I had felt a high regard for him but I did not. I had met and observed him, you see, while he visited here at Eisenstein with your father the Count during your engagement. Indeed I was party to some of their discussions, particularly as regarded the restoration of the old North Mill. If you will forgive my saying so, for all his handsome appearance, his wealth and grand title, he did not have my respect. However I was soon to thank the grace of God for turning me from the abyss, for my father's fall was but three days later. I would never have wanted him, or Kitty, to face what was to come without me."

"I am so sorry, Reynard."

"It is all right, Hilda. Everard Manx is at peace and I like to think he has rejoined my mother. As for myself, life has been painful before and at some time in the future no doubt must be painful again for one reason or another, yet I have much hope."

Drawing the back of his hand to my cheek, I asked, "So now have you told me all your secrets?"

"Not yet." From an inside pocket of his vest, he withdrew a small red volume with the sign of the cross embossed in gold. "There is this. It was my mother's. My father, from his dying bed, instructed me on where he had hidden it. He said he had been tempted many times to burn it but he felt it was not his right to do so. He begged me to destroy it. He said it bore the power to draw all Europe into war."

"And does it?"

"Oh yes, I rather think so. From the day it first came into my hand, I have carried it always safely upon my person while feeling it might combust at any moment and send flames shooting from my pocket."

He handed me the little book. I opened it. The name "Irina Adler" was written inside the cover in a delicate script. "But how," I asked, "could Psalms be the cause of war?"

"It is not the Psalms which are the problem."

On looking further, I discovered a folded sheet of paper between the pages. "That," he said. "Look at it."

He was silent as I opened out the paper and read through every word of what was written there. It was a marriage document, signed and witnessed at Wintenberg, attesting to the joining in holy matrimony of "Irina Melisande Adler, spinster" and a Mr. Axel Stefan von Turmen.

"You see," he said, placing his fingertip beneath the

date, "This was two days prior to the disaster which took the lives of the elder princes of Gothe-Saxeberg."

"Irina Adler was your mother."

"Yes."

"Why, then, Flavia and her brother Karl, the Crown Prince of Gothe-Saxeburg, are . . . "

"The illegitimate issue of a bigamous marriage. A circumstance which applies to my sister Kitty as well."

"When Mr. Manx married your mother, did he know?"

"Of the crime he was committing? Oh yes, I'm sure he did. He had always been completely in love with my mother and there was nothing he would not have done for her. But Turmen did not know, you see, that she was to bear his child. It was when he returned to visit Zenda several years later, accompanied by his royal wife, the Princess Maria Elphberg, he chanced to see my mother in the town. With me. He saw by my appearance I was his son. In the meantime, Maria had given birth to Flavia's brother Karl Stefan von Turmen who has since become the Crown Prince. My mother was expecting Kitty and Princess Maria similarly expectant of Flavia. The two couples met privately and swore to a pact of secrecy for the protection of everyone involved. A settlement of funds was also offered to my father, meaning Mr. Manx, for my upkeep, but he thought safer not to accept it and assured the Prince it would not be necessary. He had the living of the Eisenstein stewardship by then, and that meeting took place in the same room in which we sat today with the Queen. I remember it, seeing the Crown Prince von Turmen and

Princess Maria in the house, though I was a very little boy and I had no real understanding of who they were, much less that their visit had to do with me. The Prince did get down on one knee and speak kindly to me, and he gave me a sweet. I do remember that."

"But was my father there?"

"Oh, no. Your father the Count knows nothing of any of this. The visit of the Crown Prince and Princess occurred while your mother was still living. The Count and Countess were residing in Strelsau."

I looked down again at the document in my hand. "Surely this must also be noted in the parish register at Wintenberg."

"Yes, very likely it lies there as a few lines among the pages of some thick and weighty tome, unremarked by anyone. That is also just another piece of paper and could be destroyed. By an agent of the Crown, for example."

"Why, then, have you kept this?"

"I have never been quite ready to let it out of my hands. I have been completely alone with it. It was all to do with you, you see. Before you married, I lived all my life in the understanding you were born far above my station. Then no sooner do you marry than I discover I am the one legitimate son of the King of Gothe-Saxeberg, of all things. But it was useless. With you married and made Duchess of Pontsylvania, what good was it to me? It gave me such pain to look at it, I could not show it to anyone, and yet I could not let it go. Though I do recall, on that one terrible night I had it in mind to make certain it went in the fire before the bailiffs took me up. But then, because you saved me, they never came."

"So what then are you? The rightful Crown Prince of Gothe-Saxeberg?"

"No, for I would not be deemed eligible to become king, my mother having been a commoner. If I were known and at large in Gothe-Saxeberg then I suppose I might be styled a duke like our Black Michael, or if not perhaps a margrave, a landgrave, a count palatine or some sort of thing. The legitimate heirs of The Blood to the thrones of Gothe-Saxeberg and Ruritania are some unwitting uncles or cousins of mine and of the late Rudolph Elphberg, and unwitting it's surely best they should forever remain. I've not pursued the question of who they might be; the Tsarina of Russia for all I know, or perhaps the Prince of Wales, the Grand Duke of Mecklenburg-Strelitz, the Crown Prince of Norway or the King of the Cannibal Isles. But really, Hilda, who would wish to be a prince or a king? These people lead absolutely horrible lives. As well you know, even you members of the peerage do not escape the curse."

"Reynard, I know your nature. Even had I not yet married, I cannot think you would have come forward with this."

"You are quite right, Hilda. I would not wreck the lives of my father, my brother and both my sisters, whilst setting off an incendiary bomb under the map of Europe, for the sake of attaining my private heart's desire. But there would have been no cause to do so. The point is, you see, my bloodline and its legitimacy are not important. To set my eyes upon this document was a revelation to me. It showed to me, Hilda, the absurdity of our age-old customs safeguarding the purity of The Blood. This paper surely cannot make me one whit a better man than my brother Karl von Turmen, the heir apparent of Gothe-Saxeburg, yet it proves I am no lesser than he, and in finally understanding this I felt the most bitter regret."

"And what did you regret?"

"I should have tried for you, Hilda. I should have tried before it was too late. I should have spoken from my heart and let you be the one to decide. Had I been fortunate in this, then even had your father set out to withhold his consent, were we in true accord with each other there are ways we could have forced the matter as I'm sure you understand. And I am well aware that Raoul's attachments to the state of bachelorhood and life abroad had become a cause of some concern, while the alliance with Pontsylvania has been of benefit to Eisenstein in a way I could in no measure have matched, yet such matters were never your responsibility. I also know your father and brother too well to imagine they ever thought to make you responsible. It was Pontsylvania who saw an opportunity, thinking to enjoy having you all obliged to him. There can be no doubt he took great pride in your beauty but I'm just as sure he had investigated every detail of the holdings, credits, debts and general situation of the family von Eisen before making his approach. He was that sort of a man and I knew it; I was certain of it yet I said nothing to you, believing I had no right, that it was not my place, and telling myself I should be happy to see you marry a better man than your cousin Klench, for in truth I cannot answer for what I might have done if I thought you were really going to marry Klench. Therefore I held so righteously humble, keeping my subservient silence, and later in hindsight would feel positively ashamed of myself for it. Though I do assure you I am entirely glad you have Max. A child, after all, requires no justification."

He took the paper from my hand and slowly ran his eyes over the words thereon. "Now there is no one left for me to show this to. Let us not speak of it again, Hilda."

"Of course not."

He crushed it into a ball, rose and tossed it on the fire. Taking up a poker, he pressed it down into the deepest heart of the flames. "There," he said. "I remain forever Reynard Manx, the common man."

"It is well," I said. "But are you not going to ask me?"

"Ask you what?"

"What my answer would have been, had you spoken from your heart."

"No," he replied, "I am not going to ask what your answer would have been. I care only for what your answer is now."

Turning from the fire, he knelt down before me on the hearth rug. He took up my left hand and gently removed the Star of Pontsylvania. Placing it on the palm of my right hand, he closed my fingers over it. "You must keep that for Max," he said, "for when he marries."

He drew a little square packet of fine white linen from

his watch pocket and began to unfold it. It was bordered with a scalloped trim of crocheted lace. I spied the monogram *HvE* delicately embroidered on one corner.

"Oh," I said, "so you really do have one of my handkerchiefs."

"You gave it to me. And here with it is the other secret thing of my mother's which I shall certainly not be putting into the fire." In the center of the handkerchief was revealed a fine gold ring of antique design, set with a sparkling oval emerald, of the deepest green and encircled with tiny white pearls. "Hilda Marie von Eisen, every moment and every hour, you have always been to my heart and my mind the brightest, the bravest and the sweetest girl ever born. This ring was the instrument of my coming into this world. The sun has not touched it for over thirty years. Now I offer it to you."

"Oh! But even though I become Madame Manx, Reynard, I shall yet remain Dowager Duchess of Pontsylvania and mother of the Duke, with all the role entails. Are you quite sure, truly, you will always find it in your heart to go through life forgiving such a terrible imposition?"

He laughed. "Ah, Hildie! Were you to sit high upon the lofty throne of Ruritania as my unfortunate sister does, I would still love and desire you above all others and for as long as you wanted me, you would have me."

With my own handkerchief yet in his hand, he tenderly blotted the tears of joy from my face. "So, Hilda?"

"Oh Reynard, my Dearest, I will always want you and

yes, oh yes! Please do honor my hand with your royal ring, to remain for as long as I live."

"Royal rings require to be kissed," he said.

"Yes, they do. Duchesses also."

Some few minutes passed. The door opened and my father stepped in. "Ah, good evening, Hilda. There you are, Manx. Good heavens! Upon my soul, I do perceive I am no doubt committing an unwelcome intrusion. I most humbly beg your pardon. I will close this door, we may let it be as I had never opened it and we'll not speak of it again."

❖ Epilogue ❖

A note attached to the back of the manuscript

LEGATION OF THE UNITED KINGDOM AND BRITISH DOMINIONS
CAIRO
KHEDIVATE OF EGYPT

Her Grace Hilda von Eisen and von Plinth
Pontsylvania House
Herrengasse 73
Strelsau
Ruritania

Sweetest Hilda,

I send this note to confirm I am in receipt of the item which you borrowed and have since returned. I am positively delighted to have it back. Although I am now packing up as my posting has been transferred to Paris, I shall make certain not to lose it in transit. I will provide to you the new address as soon as it is determined. I do hope you will visit. It is said the trains are good. God bless you.

Yours most sincerely,
James Woodbury

❖ The End ❖

Appendix I

For the uninitiated:
Highlights from *The Prisoner of Zenda*,
by Anthony Hope (1894)

A memoir in the first person by Rudolf Rassendyll, a "well-bred" but idle English gentleman of independent means, younger brother of Lord Burlesdon. Burlesdon's wife urges him to find something worthwhile to do with himself but he doesn't see the point. We learn that Rassendyll has red hair and a distinctive nose, features said to crop up in the family once in a generation. These red-haired Rassendylls resemble the Elphbergs, royal family of Ruritania. Historically, there's reason to suspect a *liaison* in England in 1733 between a visiting Ruritanian Crown Prince and Amelia, Countess of Burlesdon. There was a duel, her husband the Count died of his wounds, the Crown Prince returned in haste to his home country and ultimately, a red-haired son was born to the widowed Countess. Rassendyll finds this explanation of his Elphbergian features amusing. His sister-in-law is embarrassed by the obvious implication the Rassendyll men who inherit the Burlesdon title, including of course her husband, are not Rassendylls by blood but instead descended from the Elphbergs through an illicit union.

She wishes the matter never to be spoken of.

The old King of Ruritania has passed and his son Rudolf Elphberg, a.k.a. King Rudolf V, is soon to be crowned in Strelsau, capitol of Ruritania. Rassendyll decides to amuse himself by attending the event. A friend seeing him off at the train station points out a fellow traveler, the widow Madame Antoinette de Mauban, a stunning heartbreaker rumored to have ambitiously set her sights on the Duke of Strelsau, known as "Black Michael," younger half brother of King Rudolf, born of their widowed father's second, and morganatic, marriage with a common woman.

Arriving in Ruritania, Rassendyll has encounters with people who behave strangely, seeming to mistake him for someone else. Having a day to kill before the coronation, he goes for a hike in the Forest of Zenda where he runs into the King himself, out hunting with two companions, a trusted old army officer, Colonel Sapt, and an elegant young gentleman, Fritz von Tarlenheim. Rassendyll and the King are gobsmacked to find that not only are they both named Rudolf, they look virtually identical. The Ruritanians also know the old story of the Crown Prince and the Countess of Burlesdon. The King welcomes Rassendyll as a cousin, inviting him to join the party for a bachelor supper at a shooting lodge where they're served by an "old woman," known to be the mother of a loyal employee of Black Michael, and a servant named Josef. Josef brings to the table a special bottle of wine sent by Michael for the King personally to drink to celebrate the impending coronation.

They all eat a lot, talk a lot, get drunk and pass out.

Sapt, Tarlenheim and Rassendyll get up early in the morning to find the King is nearly comatose. Black Michael's special gift bottle had been drugged, presumably to stop the coronation from happening and disgrace the King, whose alcoholic tendencies are well known. They ride off to Strelsau, leaving the King to sleep it off in the cellar of the shooting lodge with Josef on guard. Distrusting the old woman, Sapt has tied her up and locked her in the coal cellar.

Sapt proposes Rassendyll can save the monarchy by impersonating the King for just a few hours during the coronation ceremony and the after-party. A nervous Rassendyll goes through with it and pulls it off. He meets the King's cousin and fiancée, Princess Flavia, a pale beauty with a pure heart and a spectacular head of hair. He also meets a stunned, chagrined Black Michael. Michael knows Rassendyll is not his brother the King, and Rassendyll know he knows, but the guilty, treasonous Michael can't do a thing about it.

Sapt, Tarlenheim and Rassendyll return to the shooting lodge by night to retrieve the King, only to find the old woman has escaped, Josef lies dead with his throat cut and the King is gone. They bury Josef quickly in an unmarked grave and head back to Strelsau. On the road in the dark they meet a party of Black Michael's men carrying tools for the purpose of burying Josef; a brief skirmish ensues and one of them is shot by Rassendyll.

Back in Strelsau, Rassendyll continues impersonating

the King. Sapt deduces Michael has abducted the King and hopes to seize the throne of Ruritania and marry Flavia, who is herself an Elphberg of the legitimate royal bloodline. Michael is far more popular than his brother and confident the country will accept his rule with Flavia as Queen and future mother of his children.

It is hoped the King's life may be spared as long as Rassendyll continues to impersonate him. Killing the King will not help Michael while Rassendyll continues to occupy the throne, but should Rassendyll quit the performance and leave Ruritania, the King is surely doomed.

Michael employs a cadre of mercenaries known as "The Six." Three of them are assigned to assassinate Rassendyll. Among these is Rupert von Hentzau, a charming, courageous and amoral high-born gentleman whose mother is said to have died of a broken heart due to his shameless dishonorable exploits.

Antoinette de Mauban, now living in sin with Black Michael in his chateau at Zenda, knows she will be cast aside if his scheme to take the throne, and Flavia, is successful. She begins to aid Rassendyll by tipping him off with anonymous notes. The writer is obviously a woman and Rassendyll can easily deduce her identity.

Rassendyll is dismayed to realize long-term impersonation of the King requires faking it as Flavia's fiancé. The King has never treated Flavia well but Rassendyll finds it impossible not to show her the courtesy and respect she obviously deserves. Taken in by the imposture, Flavia believes ascending to the throne has inspired the King to turn over a new leaf. Inevitably, they fall in love as Rassendyll struggles to walk a fine line between being kind to Flavia and insulting her honor by taking advantage of her believing him to be Rudolf Elphberg.

It's discovered the King is alive and held prisoner in the old medieval castle at Zenda next to Black Michael's chateau. Rassendyll conducts a solo midnight commando recon mission, swimming the moat and stabbing to death a guard in an anchored boat, an act he mentions he's really not proud of (though he seems to get over it quickly). He determines the King is chained in a chamber fitted up with a chute through which his weighted corpse can be dispensed right to the bottom of the moat immediately the moment it becomes necessary. He is guarded around the clock in rota by members of "The Six."

Further bloody skirmishing reduces the number of "The Six" down to four with Hentzau among the survivors. Hentzau, who addresses Rassendyll as "The Play Actor," approaches him with a proposition. He will provide inside assistance with a rescue raid on the castle, but the outcome is to include the deaths of both the King and Black Michael. This will allow Rassendyll to keep the throne and Flavia. It will also clear the field for Hentzau's goal of making Antoinette de Mauban his next conquest, an end he has been already hotly pursuing for some time, increasingly irritating Black Michael while failing to win over Antoinette. A disgusted Rassendyll refuses this dishonorable offer.

The King's health is known to be deteriorating under

the harsh conditions of his captivity and it is feared he cannot survive much longer. A desperate rescue mission is planned. After a long strategizing conference, Rassendyll visits a pensive, anxious Flavia. She places a ring on his hand. In return, he gives her his pinky ring, a gold band engraved with the Rassendyll family motto, *Nil Quae Feci*. (Literal translation: "I have done nothing." How Anthony Hope intended this to be interpreted: a matter of endless speculation/debate.) He asks her to always wear it "even though you wear another when you are queen." Flavia replies, "this I will wear til I die and after."

Black Michael alone is said to possess the key needed to release the drawbridge to the castle, which is always withdrawn at night. Rassendyll will again swim the moat. An inside confederate is to allow Sapt and others to enter the chateau at exactly 2.00 am, at which time Antoinette de Mauban will lure Michael from his private apartments and into their hands by crying out in her room, pretending Rupert is assaulting her. Sapt, Tarlenheim and their men will take the drawbridge key from Michael, thus gaining access to join Rassendyll in an assault on the castle.

Rassendyll, arriving first alone and treading water in the moat, observes Hentzau slipping silently out of the castle and swimming across to the chateau where he actually does proceed to commit a surprise intrusion upon Antoinette in her *boudoir* (presumably while dripping all over the carpet). She calls out for help. Michael rushes to her aid, is wounded by Hentzau's blade, and himself calls for help. As other members of the household converge upon him, Rupert jumps from Antoinette's window into the moat.

Rassendyll, assuming the plan has been spoiled and he's on his own, enters the castle and engages the remaining three members of "The Six" in a furious fight to the death. The King, though chained to the wall, wasted and delirious, manages to give assistance but also sustains a sword cut to his head. A physician who had been brought in to attend to the King is unfortunately slain in the melee. Rassendyll is wounded but he prevails and the King survives. Rassendyll then steps outside to find Hentzau has deployed the drawbridge. (Some perplexity intrudes at this spot. Let us move on.) He stands in the middle of it facing the chateau, shouting for Black Michael to come forth and finish fighting it out with him.

Instead a hysterical Antoinette emerges, screaming that Michael is dead. She appears *en deshabille* in a white robe, her long hair streaming down. She carries a revolver, presumably Michael's, meaning to shoot Hentzau; she fires the gun once but doesn't come remotely close to hitting him. Hentzau flippantly states her beauty has already done him a lot more harm than her marksmanship will ever do. As she struggles to calm and steady herself enough to take aim for a better shot, making what Rassendyll paternalistically describes as "a wonderful effort," Hentzau bows to her, declares "I cannot kill where I have kissed," and jumps yet again into the moat. He swims away to climb out of the water at a safe distance. Although wounded, Rassendyll pursues him, first swimming and then running. He comes upon Rupert stopping a young farm girl (who is up very early indeed) and commandeering her horse, though he charms her and gives her some money. They have a conversation; Rassendyll attacks and slashes Hentzau's cheek (no doubt leaving him with a highly fashionable dueling scar) but then collapses, exhausted and bleeding, at Hentzau's mercy and prepared to die.

Meanwhile Sapt and his men have arrived and are storming the chateau as Fritz von Tarlenheim rides in search of Rassendyll. He arrives just in time, brandishing a pistol. Hentzau rides away. Tarlenheim fires after him but only succeeds in shooting the sword out of his hand (not bad). Tarlenheim refuses to chase Hentzau, instead staying to look after his wounded friend. Rassendyll muses on his mixed feelings about Hentzau, describing him as "reckless and wary, graceful and graceless, handsome, debonair, vile and unconquered."

Flavia hears the King is at Zenda, wounded and ill. She hastens to join him, traveling in a coach escorted by guardsmen. Sapt tells Flavia the King is inside the chateau and bedridden. Rassendyll attempts to hide outdoors but Flavia is brought to him by a little girl who believes him to be the King. Flavia, finally realizing the man she loves and Rudolf Elphberg are not the same person, swoons from the shock and falls insensible into his arms. Leaving her in the care of others, he slinks away in shame.

Rassendyll visits the recovering King, who is grateful for his rescue and the preservation of the monarchy but has yet to give much thought to what may have gone on with Flavia while Rassendyll was standing in for him. The King would like to keep Rassendyll around but his advisors insist this is not a good idea. Rassendyll must leave Ruritania.

Flavia meets alone with Rassendyll one last time; they share an interlude of alternating bliss and anguish. They consider eloping but conclude their dream of happiness together would be doomed in reality, hopelessly tainted by their inevitable shame.

Rudolf Rassendyll returns home to England, leaving Flavia stuck with her royal duty to marry Rudolf Elphberg.

I gathered her to me and kissed her lips.

Rassendyll slips a toe over the line with Princess Flavia
before he leaves her "forever."

Appendix II

For the uninitiated:
Highlights from *Rupert of Hentzau*,
by Anthony Hope (1898)

A memoir in the first person, by Fritz von Tarlenheim, who has remained the devoted friend of Rudolf Rassendyll. Flavia, formerly Princess and now Queen, has been married to King Rudolf V for three years. Rassendyll remains a bachelor in England. The King has become more miserable to live with than ever since the trauma of his imprisonment by Black Michael. Anxious, moody and petulant, he is descending into paranoia. He has developed dark suspicions in hindsight about Rassendyll and Flavia. No child has been produced by the royal union and Tarlenheim describes Flavia's life as being "worse than a widow." Tarlenheim has married his sweetheart Helga von Strofzin, one of Flavia's ladies in waiting. The sorrows of Flavia and Rassendyll are all the more pitiable in comparison to their happiness.

Tarlenheim and Rassendyll have been meeting once a year at some remote hostelry, outside the borders of Ruritania where they are unlikely to be recognized. Flavia sends with Tarlenheim a single rose to be given to Rassendyll along with a message consisting of "only three words." Rassendyll then writes a note in three words for Tarlenheim to bring back to Flavia.

Rupert von Hentzau is campaigning for a pardon from the King so he can return to Ruritania and reclaim the property, funds, and status he has lost in exile. His younger cousin, Count Lazau-Rischenheim, tries to intercede on his behalf. The King refuses to hear anything about reconciliation with Hentzau.

As Tarlenheim prepares for his next trip to meet Rassendyll, a desperate Flavia insists she must send an actual letter "only once" and she hopes for a letter in return. She intends to say goodbye forever and end all communication with Rassendyll, hoping this may in time prove less painful.

Tarlenheim has hired a servant named Bauer who is, unbeknownst to him, a spy in the pay of Hentzau and an eavesdropper on Tarlenheim's private conversations with Helga concerning Flavia. Bauer arranges the theft of Tarlenheim's luggage from the baggage compartment of the train, but Flavia's letter is in Tarlenheim's inside breast pocket. Tarlenheim continues the journey with only his portmanteau. On disembarking from the train, he hears a motley crowd of men have just recently gotten off a local train, hired every single cab at the station and been driven away in them, thus completely clearing the station yard of cabs. It's after dark but Tarlenheim has no choice but to walk to the inn. At a desolate spot along the route, he is ambushed by a gang of men led by Hentzau, beaten and left unconscious in the road. Hentzau rifles his portmanteau and his pockets, triumphantly finding and taking Flavia's letter.

Tarlenheim is carried to the inn where Rassendyll finds him. Rassendyll is accompanied by his trusted English manservant, James. Tarlenheim recalls Hentzau's cousin Rischenheim has an audience scheduled with the King in two days. Rassendyll deduces Hentzau will send him with a copy of Flavia's treasonous love letter to show the King, offering to turn over the original letter in return for Hentzau's reinstatement. James stays to care for Tarlenheim while he recovers and Rassendyll immediately rides for Ruritania, intent on foiling Rischenheim's mission and retrieving the letter.

Rassendyll is reunited with Colonel Sapt and Queen Flavia at Zenda where the King's court is currently in residence. A young officer of the Royal Guards, Lieutenant Bernenstein, walks in on the scene of this reunion and is confused until Sapt decides to just tell him the truth and order him to keep his mouth shut. Bernenstein swears his loyalty belongs entirely to Flavia, kneeling at her feet and declaring he would die for her.

Rischenheim is required to come at an earlier time for his royal audience. On arriving, he is directed into a meeting with Rassendyll impersonating the King. Rassendyll succeeds temporarily but the real King has changed so much in the last few years, Rischenheim figures out before the end of the interview he's talking to Rassendyll. Sapt holds him at gunpoint for some time, including as he sits down to breakfast with the real King Rudolf. Rischenheim struggles to choke down his food while Sapt stands behind the King's chair aiming a pistol at him. Rassendyll is also present in the breakfast room hiding behind the window draperies. Following this nerve-wracking repast, Sapt and Rassendyll take the copy of Flavia's letter from Rischenheim along with a telegram stating only the street address of a house in Strelsau. Rassendyll deduces this telegram is from Hentzau and means he's back in Ruritania.

An attempt to lure Hentzau into a trap at a hunting lodge goes horribly wrong when he arrives not to find Rassendyll and his allies lying in wait as had been intended, but instead the actual King Rudolf in residence. Hentzau has been duped into believing he has been called to an audience with the King to discuss Flavia's letter and a potential bargain for his reinstatement. The paranoid King, knowing nothing of any such arrangement, is shocked and terrified by Hentzau's unexpected arrival. A confused interaction at cross-purposes ensues. Ultimately Hentzau is attacked by Boris, the King's loyal and protective boarhound. Things go rapidly downhill from there with a perplexed Hentzau obliged to shoot the dog, the King and his attendants in self-defense. He then rides off, his plans in ruins and wondering what the hell just happened. Sapt and Tarlenheim arrive at the scene of this bloodbath to find one man, the King's forester, still breathing. Although mortally wounded, he manages to give an account of the massacre and name Hentzau as the killer before he expires

Flavia takes note of the plight of the youthful and now miserable Count Lazau-Rischenheim, his future destroyed by his complicity in the exploits of his persuasive and reckless elder cousin, now a regicide. She requests and receives his oath of fealty and then grants him clemency, taking him into her retinue.

Rassendyll confronts the desperate Hentzau in the vile garret in Strelsau where he has been hiding out. They agree to fight a gentlemanly duel with rapiers while Flavia's letter waits on the mantlepiece, just inches away from a fire that could destroy it, as a prize for the winner. Hentzau, ultimately disarmed after a stiff fight, tries to cheat by drawing a pistol from the back of his waistband. Rassendyll grapples with him and slowly, slowly manages to turn the muzzle of the gun to Hentzau's own heart. Hentzau, finally having lost all hope, pulls the trigger. Rassendyll reads through Flavia's letter and then consigns it to the flames. Others in the house have seen Rassendyll both arriving and leaving at the scene of Hentzau's demise, believing him to be the King.

Sapt admits he has gone back to the hunting lodge and burned it down with the body of the King still inside. The death of the King having not yet been disclosed to the public, this leaves the way open for Rassendyll to resume impersonating him, an outcome Sapt is hoping for.

Rassendyll's small circle of allies urge him to marry Flavia in a private ceremony and stay on to rule Ruritania. Rassendyll is torn between his great love for Flavia and his feeling that a secret marriage with the Queen and a life lived out on the throne pretending to be Rudolf Elphberg would be dishonorable. He paces alone in the palace garden by moonlight, deliberating while Flavia and his friends watch and wait. At last Rassendyll comes to meet them on the terrace, about to announce his decision. Flavia is so overwhelmed with anxiety at this moment, her legs are failing and Tarlenheim has to hold her up. Rassendyll however never gets the chance to speak. Hentzau's loyal henchman Bauer, hot for revenge, has climbed over the palace wall. He steps out from behind a tree with a revolver in hand. At the moment he appears, Bernenstein rushes forward, drawing a cutlass as he thrusts Flavia out of the line of fire. He strikes a blow at Bauer in the same instant Bauer shoots Rassendyll in the back. Bauer tries to escape while turning back to fire more shots, but Bernenstein, heedless of the flying bullets, chases him down and finishes him off.

Rassendyll, carried to a bed in the palace, declines to reveal what decision he had intended to announce but instead states, "God has decided." He reaffirms his love for Flavia and dies. The King's charred corpse in the hunting lodge is reported to be the body of Rassendyll while the man assassinated at the palace is reported to have been the King.

Rudolf Rassendyll's remains are entombed in the Cathedral of Strelsau among the Princes of the Royal House of Elphberg. Queen Flavia is left to rule Ruritania alone.

Author's Final Note

The first time I read *Rupert of Hentzau* (at around age 14), I naturally hoped all the way through that Sir Anthony had regretted the sad and frustrating conclusion of *The Prisoner of Zenda,* or perhaps heard too many complaints about it, and *Hentzau* was the re-do that would bring Rudolf Rassendyll and Flavia together at last. It seemed obvious this must be our destination and indeed, after many a twist and turn, we were nearly there. All the obstacles between them had been swept away, and then, after much anticipation . . . the rug whipped out from under the hopeful reader in just the last few pages. Oh, but of course. It was Purity of Honor, not love, happiness or even life which required service in the end, even if it did (or did it, Mr. Rassendyll?) require a rather contrived intervention from God to keep Flavia and her first choice of Rudolfs without stain (well, other than all those bloodstains all over the map of Ruritania). So there you have it. The King is Dead; Long Live the Queen; and if one prefers a different outcome, one may write one's own book.

About the Author

In the course of a tumultuous life, Kristin Rose has demonstrated the capacity to birth and raise a child, type 70 words a minute, supervise difficult persons, shoot a gun, drive a stick shift, deploy a fire extinguisher and hook up jumper cables correctly. She has known success in catching fish from various boats on fresh and salt waters. She knows what to do with said caught fish. She has been a martial artist and a belly dancer. She once grabbed a coworker in the kitchen of a Howard Johnson's restaurant by the collar while whispering graphic threats of violence. (He never bothered her again.) She has towed an Opel Kadett with a dead battery on a dirt road in the woods from behind the wheel of a bottled propane delivery truck. She always lives with cats. Her skill set includes theatrical and dance costuming, quilting, restoring antique trunks, wallpapering, gardening and fixing up old houses. She admits full responsibility for the existence of the play script, *The Witch of Love*. She has not jumped out of a plane. She lives in Windsor, Vermont.

Images

Cover design by Betsy Alexander and the author.

Cover photos: Antique *verdure* tapestry on display at Castle of the Teutonic Order, Malbork, Poland. Crown Princess Maude of Norway in evening dress (*née* Princess Maude of Wales, later Queen Maude of Norway).

Title page: Heraldic doodle by the author.

Author's Note illustrations: Cover design for American edition of *The Prisoner of Zenda*, Henry Holt & Co., 1895; artist Will Phillip Hooper. Frontispiece from a 1921 edition of *The Prisoner of Zenda;* artist Howard Ince.

Appendix I: Illustration for *The Prisoner of Zenda*, 1898; artist Charles Dana Gibson.

Chapter vignettes: Sourced from The Old Design Shop blog, Scott Foresman collection on Wikimedia Commons, or Rawpixel Ltd. *via* Wikimedia Commons; or by the author.